MW00480058

The Nine Lives Of Felix The Tomcat

Felix the Tomcat

And M. P. Frank

Disclaimer

© 2022 Michael Patrick Frank and Felix the Tomcat. All rights reserved.

This book is a work of fiction. Any names, characters, companies, organizations, places, events, locales, and incidents are either used in a fictitious manner or are fictional. Any resemblance to actual persons, living or dead, actual companies or organizations, or actual events is purely coincidental.

ISBN 978-1-7388165-1-4

For rights and permissions, please contact:

Michael Patrick Frank and Felix the Tomcat

Michealpatrickfrankwriter@gmail.com

FelixtheTomcat@felixthetomcat2022.blog

Printed in the United States

Thanks

To my incredible friends...my gang... Slick, Goldenboy, Hank, Gloomer, Rosa, lovely Afrodite.... And even that asshole V-Dome. Sincerely, Felix the Tomcat

To my amazing partner, Linda, and my loyal friends and family, and my amazing four grandkids. I hope someday, when your parents let you read this, you will chuckle and say, "Wow, Pop was a trip!" Thank you to Joseph Idaye at Upwork for formatting this book and cover design for Kindle. M.P. Frank

See our website: FelixtheTomcat2022.blog/

> "Time spent with cats is never wasted." —Sigmund Freud

Table of Contents

Chapter 1

Operation Foul Swoop

"A dog has an owner...a cat has a staff."—Anon

My muscular chest broke through the waves of underbrush in the tropical rainforest, like the prow of a Roman galleon. My tawny orange, brown, and white fur with black rosette markings blended in with the dappled shadows of the forest flora. I was stalking a yummy-looking mule deer. With a lunge my awesome haunches propelled me through the air, landing on the deer's back. I sunk my 18 razored claws into the thick brown coat of my prey and bared my vicious 2" jaguar choppers ready to pierce the quivering mammal's skull.

It screamed, "Let go of me, you Fudding cat!" and delivered a vicious left uppercut to my snout, splayifying me on the nasty shag carpet.

1

I had been snoozing in bed with Dakota for a couple of hours, snuggled between her magnanimous breasts. She took 2 Ambeens at 4 PM trying to catch a snooze prior to returning to night shift at the Seven-Eleven.

My thoughts kept wandering back to that awe-inspiring 'BIG CAT SPECIAL' on Animal Planet. I watched it yesterday for the twelfth time. I love that program.

I got unlimited TV access living here. Fishface always left the TV on and the remotes lying all over when he was either drunk, stoned or sleeping, which constituted 89.7% of his empty existence. I was slick with remotes.

Fishface got a VA pension for catching PTFSD in 'The Storm'. Since then, he just lays around the house. Loafing-not living... like a no-income-poop, all moody and lazy. PTFSD stands for Post Transatlantic Fu**ing Stress Disease... if you didn't know that.

I saw a CNN special on PTFSD. It was mighty catchy out there in that big sandbox they called I-Rock. Many of the soldiers over there caught PTFSD- very infectifyed. It can make people act strange: withdrawn, depressed, anxious, and angry... like Fishface.

Back to the 'BIG CAT SPECIAL'. Really, to be fair, I should have been a jaguar. Now, a jaguar is A REAL CAT. An Apex Predator: superfast, streamlined, fabulous orange, brown and white fur with black spots in Rosette patterns (like me), 18 seriously gnarly retractable two-inch claws (5 claws per front foot and 4 per back foot), massive jaws and razor-teeth with a skull-crushing bite. Jaws with up to 300 pounds of bite pressure and no shit from no-buddy!

In my mind I am a Jaguar... the sports package. Hey, I got 96.5% of the same damn DNA as that husky feline machine. Just a little tweek of my jeans (spread over my 38 chromysomes) and Bazinga! I got it all: the muscle, the speed (35-40 mph), more good looks and, definitely, all the meat I can chase, bite, chew and swallow! No more damn dogs yapping at me in the alley and no feisty raccoons chasing me (they are the worst!) and no more goddam 'owners'!

'Stop fanatasizing... you twat!' Felix, your fate was casted in stones at conscription. I am what I am. I am going to have to live in this beautiful sleek jaguar-colored coat, with my threatening canines, my 'not-so-shabby' junk, my beautiful mind, my sharpened sense of humor, and my healthy self-image... and cope. But, in my mind, I am a jaguar.

So, you think I might be a little full of myself? Well, OK... take a fine-lookin tomcat (felis catus) with a brilliant mind and give that cat hyperthymesia (superb ottobiographic recall... the Learning Channel). Some people call that a photographic memory. Now, give that brainiac tomcat unlimited access to TV (with the remote): Nature Channel, Animal Planet, CNN, History Channel,

Discovery Channel, and Jeoperdy Reruns. Congratulations, you have cloned yourself one super-bright feline. With my hyperthymesia I could not <u>force</u> myself to forget anything! I remember everything: smells, sounds, hunts, sex, events, names, scenes, faces, words, sentences, quotes, and ideas… everything, in antagonizing detail.

The average housecat is, well, average. Cute, furry, possibly… but sneaky, lazy, boring and generally stupid as a boot! And totally narcissifyed… totally! Generally, apart from Tomcats, housecats are a bunch of losers. (in Chapter 26 I will explain how that happened over 10000 years of evolution. Read on.)

I was the eggception, me, Felix the Tomcat (I named myself after felis catus). I was both a treat to the eyes and a mighty fine specimen of a Tomcat. (the Apex Predator of New Zealand, 2021).

EDITORS NOTE: Dear readers. I am a cat lover. I do not share Felix's low opinion of house cats or his high opinion of himself. Please send your hate mail directly to Felix at FelixtheTomcat2022@outlook.com. Leave me the hell out of it.

EDITOR'S NOTE: without their dentures, neither Dakota nor Fishface could pronounce the consonant diagraph 'ck' as in 'mucking' or 'trucking' and therefore those verbs sounded like 'mudding', 'trudding' or occasionally 'fudding'. Hey, don't blame me!

"You fudding Idiot!" screamed the edentulous Fishface from the living room. "Rothmans Burger!"

He continued, "my Fudding Aunt Gwen can throw better than that!" I did not approve of Fishface's vulgarudity.

A beer bottle smashed against the wall. He never threw the full ones. It was Monday Night Football... 8 or 12 beers, a pack of Marlboro's, 6 or 8 joints while glued to the tube... Football Night right here in downtown Pittsburgh As usual, he was reclined in his stupid burgundy Bark-a-lunger... watching the Steelers lose. I hate that crappy team. They are a home team disadvantage.

Fishface was getting on my nerves. Monday nights often ended poorly... for Fishface.

What a weird game: huge human beans with wide shoulders and tight pants, bright sweaters with numbers on them, funny, shiny hats with little cages on the front, and weird-looking grass. All of them yelling at the guys with the black-and-white tops.

Once in a while, they all stop yelling and they all bend over ... and then they run into each other to knock everybody down on the grass- the big dopes. And I cannot follow that goofy, pointy-ended ball that rolls funny. The whole thing is bizarrifyed. Obviously, football is another alcohol-dependent human-bean activity (ADHBA). There are always about a billion other silly human beans, wearing the same bright sweaters, sitting on their butts yelling and drinking beers. Some of them paint big letters on their chests, take their shirts off and sit there, freezing their butts off in frosty Pittsburg. The morons at the game are just like Fishface but without the ugly burgundy Bark-a-lunger. He got that nasty thing at a garage sale and calls it 'the mother ship'.

Sorry, I divurge. I had no intention of letting Fishface disturb another dreamy evening between Dakota's breasts without some correctifying action (payback).

I watched a program on the History Channel about this 600-year-old Chinaman, General Sun Sue. I don't know if he could fight but he could sure quote and he knows how to make damn good chickun. Anyway, as a bit of a general myself, I've adopted many of his smarter ideas into my warfare stratagems. I launchify frequent squirmishes against cats, dogs, rats, mice, squirrels, raccoons, and, of course, the one human bean who is my genesis, Fishface. I turn to the General for good tactical advice in times of action.

Rejected from between Dakota's breasts, I had a nice stretch on the shag carpet and buffed my claws with my raspy tongue. (actually covered with tiny barbs...Animal Planet) I shook my sleek jaguarish coat and tippy-toed quietly into the living room. Dakota always left the door ajar for my convenience in case nature called. She forced Fishace to build a cat-flap (an invention by Sir Isaak Newton) for me, from an old truck mudflap, in the kitchen door so I could go outside whenever I fancied. Dakota liked me.

There I was: free, single, brilliant, fed most of the time, and living in a crappy flat in downtown Pittsburg with a classic under-retriever, Fishface, and his stat-ue-esk, whopper-size wife, Dakota, who was mostly all right.

Fishface was splayed out in the burgundy Bark-a-lunger like a pregnant manatree, a large Florida sea mammal. (Animal Planet). His feet were up, his head tilted back, watching the tube. He had a reefer in his right hand, a cigarette in his left hand and a beer between his knees. He was a Rollin Rock guy. He worked at the beer factory before The Storm where he caught PTFSD. He claims the factory gave him free beer... a '2-4' every Friday at quittin time. He probably stole it. I was a Bud cat myself.

I hopped up to my military observation plat-form, a tacky for-Mika shelf on the wall up about 6 feet above and behind the burgundy Bark-a-lunger, to survey the field of battle and assess my enemy's strengths. Fishface was oblivamous to my presence at his 12 o'clock. I shared his weed smoke with him, second-hand. Now, what would General Sue do?

"Let your plans be as dark and as impenetra-ble as night, and when you move, fall like a thunderbolt" (The General).

"When the strike of a hawk breaks the body of its prey, it is because of timing." (the G). I loved that Chi-naman.

It was time for 'Operation Foul Swoop." Fishface appeared to be unconscious or dead. I had a few too many wiffs of secondhand weed smoke and drifted off.

When I awoke, the game was still on... 4th quarter with 2 minutes to go, Skins 36 to Steelers 6. Fishface appeared to be dead. This being my ottobiography (written while I am still alive) allow me put on my arthur's hat and properly describe my genesis... Fishface: balding badly, pudgy bulbous nose, fringe of grubby dirty brown hair with a stubby ponytail, chubby red face, wispy nicotine-stained beard, yellowed teeth, foul breath, stinky charmpits, 24- pack beer belly, tattoos all over (my favorite, 'I am a US Maureen,' big, on his left arm), ragged-looking Steelers shirt #7, the Storm pants, and, of course, his constant footwear, the tattified Army boots from the Storm. Fishfacehad a face like a river carp. His shirt was off because he was sweating.

Fishface was surrounded by 8 empty beer bottles, shards of glass from #5, the one he tossed, and a half-full brewski #9, sitting on the shag carpet. Brew #10 was tucked in his crotch. He was snoring...a rumbling bass drone, punctuated by the odd fart. STRIKE TIME!

With an ear-piercing, ban-she scream, I launched 'Operation Foul Swoop' and myself from my military observation platform into the heart of battle.

"All is fair in love and war." (the G).

I landed, nailing the strike zone- the middle ground of his flabby chest. I dug 18 staccato scratcheroonies into his bare chest with my razor-claws, then nipped his nose with my incisors and then crunched down on his WEINER with my four needle-nosed canine teeth. Blood spurted forth from his nose like a geezer in Yellowstone Park.

I escaped with a deft front flip, hurtling high over his legs and landing elegruntly on the filthy grey shag in front of the burgundy Bark-a-lunger. Whew! The hawk had struck.

Fishface was having afroplexie: red face, gasping, wheezing, gurgling, grunting, shaking and speechless ....

A horse female voice eruptifyed from the bedroom," Fishface! Y'asshole!" she explained, "What are you doing to that fudding cat? Are you teasing him again?" (Dakota's teeth were having a swim in a glass beside her bed)

Arthurs note: You see, reader, everyone called him Fishface... if you met him you would too, even if you were a Jehovah's Witless.

I was standing on the shag beside the Bark-a-lunger... just waiting to see what was going to happen next. I could not suppress a wee, sheikish grin.

To my genuine surprise, Fishface, who had been glaring at me in a hostilified manner suddenly smiled and reached out his right hand towards me, in a gentle fashion. Surrender? Was this surrender already? I blushed.

"I bet the little fella just wants a nice bowl of warm cream. Come here, little man", he whispered in a voice that would curdle peanut butter. Maybe he was afraid of Dakota.

"Supreme excellence consists of breaking the enemy's resistance without fighting." (the G)

I edged toward Fishface and gave his nicotine-stained fingers a quick swipe with my raspy tongue. Hmmm, no problemo. Then, I rubbed the sleek black-orange rosettified fur of my neck cautiously against his palm. Hmmm, no problemo.

'Ya gotta give a little to get a little.' (Felix the Tomcat)

"Bring on the cream! "I purred.

"One cartload of the enemy's provisions is equivalent to twenty of one's own." (the General)

Instantly, Fishface's soft-stroking right hand morphified into a vice-grip around my midsection. He had brutal grip strength from all that beer drinking.

In a flash, he yanked me up into the air, like a live grenade, circled me behind his right ear and hurled me, in a perfect spiral, across the living room and out the open kitchen window.

Even General Sue must have lost a squirmish or two... of course he did! War, war... and more war.

"One mark of a great soldier is that he fights on his own terms or fights not at all." (The G)

Chapter 2

The Motherfucking Racoon .... The Art of War

"One cat's garbage is another cat's buffet." —*Felix the Tomcat*

I awoke in a garbage pail. There was a heavenly aroma of fish. The fish-munger down the block was a Moreman: more wives, more sex, more kids ...you know that bunch. Anyway, the fish guy didn't know that the Pope had called off fish-on-Fridays. God told the Pope (a good Catholick) that the fish supply was dwindlifying, I guess. Anyway, everyone quit eatin fish on Fridays. Every Sunday night, the Moreman dude had to toss out all the extra fish he kept ordering for Friday. I got to eat them. I liked to let them age in the garbage pail a day or two... to enhancify the delicate flavor. Monday night delight.

Arthur's note: If I manage to offend any individual, race, or religous group in this, my ottobiography, please just hang on and keep reading… I will likely offend everyone else before long. Cheers, Felix the Tomcat.

There I was in the garbage can, chowing down some fish Goodies: a couple of livers, brains, hearts, lots of yummy intestines, and a tasty kidney or two. When it came to fish, I was a con-a-sewer.

I was in the garbage can snarfifying fish and thinking about my current life. My 'nom de gare' was 'That Fucking Cat' (TFC). TFC was a name that suited my feistifyed personality and romantified nature. TFC was also my 'nom d'amoor', my loverboy name. I decided to Frenchifry my language a few months ago. With my photographic memory and by watching Rosetta's Stones on the Learning Channel, I picked up conversational French in a coupla weeks. Speaking French has really helped my love-life. French gave me 'allure'. Just mutter a little 'Tu es bellisimo!' or 'Je t'adoor!' to a female cat in heat (Queen) and they jump you before you can jump them. French has turned me into a virtual 'love machine'. I also discovered that a litte old fish scent on the fur worked like Axe in the charmpits, along with my natural hot furrmones.

Feeling a wee stuffed, I peeped my head out of the garbage can to recon the alley where Fishface had tossed me.

A humungous mother-of-a-raccoon looked back at me out of her one good eye. She was sitting on the pavement in the middle of the alley 7 feet away staring right at me... grinning.

"Oh shit! I hate raccoons!" (Felix the Tomcat). Raccoons are super-speedy, agile and plenty-nasty and they got nothing against cat meat. I did not want her sharing a garbage pail with me. (I am not a racist.)

"There is no instance of a nation benefiting from prolonged warfare"' (the G)

The General and I concurred on that. Attacking that Raccoon mother was not an option.

I leaped upward with a complex, twisting motion to a-light on the top of the alley fence. The raccoon sprang through the air, right on my tail. Skeddewdling down the fence, I cat-a-pulted myself across the alley to land on the shed roof in the neighboor's yard. Look out Cirque du Chalet. The damn raccoon followed me, mucho fleet-of-foot and no stranger to astrobatics. Damn, she was fast! In spite of one eye, her depth perspection was uncanny. (Animal Planet)

Leaping back down to the pavement, I flipped on my after-burners and took off, jinking back and forth. I tore down the alley (31 mph) to get her off my tail. She was still gaining ground!

As she sunk her teeth into my gorgeous black,white and orange tail I dove through the mud-flap / cat-door... to safety. No way could she follow me... too big.

I observed that my tail was still being chomped on. That damn raccoon must have been all fur and teeth and hair... or she just finished six months with Jimmy Craig. Further defensive manuvers were required.

When the raccoon briefly eased her dental grip on my tail, to move north to my butt, I made my next move. Scooting over the dirty carpet, I leaped, howling, right over Fishface who was having his post-game nap. With ease, I flew over Fishface, over the burgundy bark-a-lunger, and briefly touched down on the shag floor.

Then I hopped up to my observation platform to plan my further strategems. Cats can jump up to six times their length. (Nature Channel)

The raccoon took the bait. She followed my every move, but lacked the necessary critical velocity and altitude to clear Fishface's massive carcass. What that racoon lacked in altitude she made up for in attitude! She pounced on Fishface's belly: clawing, spitting, whining, biting, twisting, and scratching. The raccoon sunk her big incisors and her four jagged canines into Fishface's nose, still slick with blood from our previous squirmish. .

'The enemy of my enemy is my friend.' (the G). I chuckled. This was way better than the Sopranos! Hopelessly outgunned, but not totally helpless, Fishface's left hand suddenly shot up and grabbed the raccoon by the tail. The ambidexterous Fishface flipped the critter skyward (he musta tossed grenades in The Storm) and whipped her round and round... faster and faster... in a dizzifying helicopter spin. The raccoon, terrified, howling and whimpering, was rendered intercontinental and peed herself. Then puked!

Fishface lost his grip on the urine-soaked tail and the raccoon spun wildly thru the air, like a boomerrang. CRASH... thru the screen of the huge box-like consular TV: Shattering glass, a flash, a loud sizzle, thick black smoke, a burst of flames ... and the nasty odor seriously frickafryed raccoon.

I held my paw to my pounding heart for a second. Respect... but no regrets!

It was time to make TFC a preciously-scarce commodity in this neighboorhood. I creptifyed, in stealth mode, toward the catflap.

While attempting my stealthified exit across the shag, I bumped into 2 large, smelly, bare feet... complete with toe-nail fungus. I looked up to see the profile of the Sierra Nevada almost concealing the once-cute face of a very disgruntified Dakota haloed by dishoveled blonde hair. Sheikishly, I grinned at her. She scowled back.

"Fishface! What are you doing to That Fudding Cat?" she yelled. She had a frying pan in her hand. Who the frying pan was for was unclear, maybe Fishface... maybe me. I crept for the cat-flap. Time for a night out on the town.

Chapter 3

A Night in the Alley and the Meaning of Life

"Tomcats have agendas.... Geniuses have philosophy."
—H. Simpson

Tomcats (that's male cats, like me, who still got gonads) are all about four things: Stalking, killing, and eating (that's one), sleeping, grooming and sex; much like the modern metro-sexual human bean. With Tomcats, add violence.

The first order of bizness for my night in the alley was to locate, stalk, kill and consume some tasty critter… hopefully, much smaller than that damn raccoon. I really wasn't sure if that raccoon incident constituted the loss of my full second life or not. I figured I better adjust my 'lives-spent' total to one-and-a-half to be on the safe side. I do not want to be short-a-life later (at 7 or 8) when I'm running short. Cats have 9 lives. (Folk fact) Too bad cats can't buy life insurance. We could clean up.

I lost my first life before I even thought about toilet-training. My ex-'owner', His Weirdness, decided to put me thru the garbage-eater, headfirst, after I peed on his scalp. Honestly, it was an innocent slip of the bladder for a kitten. His Weirdness had no conscription of what 'territorial instinct' meant. I was simply obeying Nature's laws. What a wuss he was! Cost me: a chunk outa my left ear, a lot of hair, and a coupla hundred deca-bells of hearing loss, and, maybe, a few points off my IQ. It cost me a life... no question. I skeedaddled out of Weirdness' place after that squirmish. That's how I wound up living with Fishface and Dakota and how my age got to be 1.5 lives. That racoon just claimed a half-life, since I basically won that fracus.

A cat has phenomenal hearing. A cat can hear in a range of 50 to 64,000 hurtz. Human beans hear 50 to 23,000 hurtz. Cats use their ears (what's left of them) like satellite dishes to focus the softest noise into their auditory apparatchuks. No kidding... even with my hearing loss, I can hear a dog scratch or a mouse fart at 100 yards.

"Psss...ffftt!" A mouse farted. The hunt was on!

I crept down the alley in stealth mode toward my wee flatulent foe. As I approached I sniffed. I could smell it too. Cats can also smell way better than humans.

Cats have over 100 million olfartry cells. Human beans have under 20 million.

If that mouse expected to see another sunrise, he (or she) had best lay off the granola. I crept down the alley...50...75...100 yards. I peered around the fence into a corner. My slit-like green eyes adjusted to the dark. That mouse was just loafing around, nibbling at some stale bread (multigrain), which had spilled out of the garbage. No wonder he had gas. He was upwind and had no inkling of my presence.

I assumed attack mode: back arched, hunches coiled, fangs glinting in the moonlight, claws bared, and launched at the little fella... like a jaguar. Bit him, tossed him, batted him around a few times... chased him, caught him, bit him, tossed him, batted him around a few times... and ... repeat the above for 7 or 8 minutes. It was like foreplay. Finally, I picked up his mangled body and swaggered down the alley. My trophy and a snack for later. I was still full of fish. Tomcats hunt for fun and exercise and food. (Nature Channel)

I sat on top of a shed and groomed my purrfect white, black, brown and orange coat. My mom was a Burmese cat, I think. I had got a bit grubby with all the fish-eating, hunting, and fighting. I licked my paws and feet, buffed my claws, smoothed my fur, and gave my strokum a quick once-over with my raspy tongue. I groomed my ears with my paws and licked my glossy, jaguar coat. I stretched, shook a few times, shimmified my sleek muscles, and rubbed some furrmones around from my neck and jaw glands on the wood around me... so other cats would leave me alone. A beautiful autumn night. Time to think about the meaning of life...

I watched a great program on TLC a few weeks ago, 'The Philosophers of the Ages and the Meaning of Life.' A bunch of British actors impersonifyed all the famous deep thinkers in history. The dudes were all sitting around in a Greek amphitheater discussing the meaning of life.

First came Pluto, a bearded dude with a white robe. He grabbed the mike. "The purpose of life is to seek enlightenment by seeking knowledge." A good start, Pluto!

Then Aristottle, in the same kinda outfit, bearded with a white robe said, "Happiness is the meaning of life... the whole aim and end human existence". Aristottle sounded like a fun guy.

Mother Teresa, the only woman present, habitually dressed in her white and blue outfit, walked over to the podium. "A life not lived for others is not a life." Maybe not so fun. Nuns got none.

Then Kamus, a serious dude wearing a dark old-fashioned overcoat, stepped to the podium. "It was previously a question of finding out whether life had to have meaning to be lived. It now becomes clear that it will be lived all the better if it has no meaning". Whew... dark.

Then Kamus piped up again, now smoking a cigarette, "The only serious question about life is whether to kill yourself or not." Ewww! Someone pass that boy the Prozac.

The other guys were all getting agitatifyed... all wanting to talk at the same time. They grouped around the podium, fighting for the mike, and getting more scrappy. All the philosophers were smoking cigarettes... even Mother T. was puffin on a stogie.

Then old Nitzkey, big walruss mustache and tiny specs, grabs the mike and yelled, "Pluto is a bore!" They all laughed. Pluto looked pissed.

Nitzkey continued, "Meaning and morals of one's life come from within oneself. The good life is everchanging, challenging, devoid of regret, intense, creative and risky." That guy thought just like a tomcat. No mention of the 'God is dead' stuff that he made his name on.

Then Chopenhiney, wearing a little tux with fuzzy tufts in his hair piped up, "Life without pain has no meaning." Everyone groaned. Right, tell that to the damn raccoon who just crunchifyed my tail.

Then Buddah, all jolly and round in an orange robe, waddled up to the mike. "We are shaped by our thoughts, we become what we think. When the mind is pure, joy follows like a shadow that never leaves."

The guys were getting downright rowdy by then... yelling, "Define thoughts? Define pure!... What does never mean?" Buddah just smiled like he ate a canary.

Next, Martin Luther, the Reformer, dressed in a black gown and a boxy-looking black hat, looking hostile, said, "FAITH tramples underfoot all reason, sense, and understanding!" Nitzkey clenched his fists and pouted like he was pondering punching the preacher, old Martin Luther, in the mouth. Everyone looked confused... more shoving broke out.

Finally, a guy sitting on a motorcycle way out on the edge of the ampitheatre cleared his throat a few times, stubbed out his cigarette and walked over to grab the mike. He was all dressed in black leather with grubby black cowboy boots. Dirty grey hair... and a face like a wolf. I thought it was Johnny Cash. I was expecting him to bust out in 'Folsum Prisin Blues.' He coughed and spat and then commented, in a raspy horse voice, "The purpose of life is to live."

The man in black walked away and climbed back on his motorcycle. Then he yelled, "And Quality... Quality!" He fired up his chopper and ripped out of the amphitheater, leaving a cloud of exhaust swirling like a dark cloud.

The other guys were whispered among themselves... "Who the hell was that man in black?" Buddha, still grinning, said, "That was Zen, the motorcycle mechanic." All the other guys were hysterifyed, laughing and slapping each other's backs. "A mechanic? What does he know?" said Aristotottle.

Before long, they all got back to arguing about what exactly 'life' was, and what 'purpose' meant, and what 'happiness was' and 'if there is a God... why didn't we see or hear something good from Him more often (what with all the earthquakes and Sunamees and other nasty shit?).' And they tried to define quality... but couldn't. The program ended with Aristottle looking like an ass because he could not explain what 'is' is.

Overall, it was a great program... deep. It made my brain Hurt. The Zen guy was fantastic... both brains and balls... just like me. And 'Quality'... I had to think about that one. I fell asleep. The noise of howling Tomcats woke me. Tomcats- that's plural. That could mean only one thing... a Queen in heat! A Tomcat emergency!

Female cats, with go-nads, are called Queens (Nature Channel). Queens go into estrus, or heat, about twice a year, sometimes more. During heat, they are 'the gift that just keeps givin,' up until they get pregnified. When they are pregnified... and all the rest of the time... it's strickly no-can-do!

When Queens are in heat they give off certain furrmones that draw every Tom from blocks away... like bears to honey. And, the queens are not exactly monogmified. Queens want plenty of sexual partners... to get pregnified. And it's all con-sexual; all part of being real cats with working go-nads. Therefore, a litter of kittens may represent a regular swimming pool of jeans. As the Nature Channel says, 'your brudder may be your uncle by anuder mudder'... or something like that. I loved 'the circle of life'.

Time was of the esscents. Using my warped speed and my sensitized sniffer I closed in on the furrmone trail, which lead me one alley over from my familiar turf. I didn't usually hang with that crowd of cats. They were genuine, downtown Pittsburg tuff-cats.

There she was! The Queen. Spikey orange fur... just prancing around the middle of the alley...tail up, mewing and purring like Madonna, but no virgin! She was one foxy-lookin Queen!

The question in the air was ripe, "Who was the Man? Who was The Alpha Tomcat?"

Grouped around, on top of the fence, looking down into the alley, were five tuff-looking Toms ... downtown Pittsburg Toms ... all strutting their stuff and staring down the other guys. All those tuff-guys had big scars, patches of missing fur, and chipped teeth. Orthodentally incorrect but plenty mean. All five of them had a total of four intact ears, not including my one good ear. The burning question was,"Could I possibly get screwed and remain alive?"

The Alpha cat suddenly declared himself, by partially amputating an ear from one of the Alpha wannabees. Three intact ears remained. I streamlined myself, making my profile smaller. The pecking order would work itself out. The Alpha Cat hopped down to the alley floor and romanced the Queen, who was hot to copulatte. The other guys were now staring at me. Baring their teeth... tails whippin back and forth. They must have thought I was a contender!

I meekly explained in Catonese (the Universal cat language), "Hey, guys! I can do Kappa, or Gamma? How about Omeega? Shit, yah! Omeega's purrfect!"

I shrugged. "No problemmo," and I waited my turn.   Finally, except for me and the Queen, the alley was empty. She was snoozing. It was time for luv!

I stud-walked up to the queen... who woke up, but was looking a bit haggard from all the continuous koitus. I whispered, "Je t'adoor, mon petite shat."

She gave me an odd look. Encouraged, I murmured, "Vous etes mucho bellisimo, mon Cherie," and rubbed my furrmoned scented neck (with just a splash of river carp) against her neck. She sneezed.

Not wanting to waste any more precious time on fore-play, I circled lazily behind her and, with gusto, mounted her. She did not object or run away or bite me. She yawned. I proceeded, with expotorential energy and… Kapoeey! E-jack-ulized. She yawned again, got up, and wandered off down the alley.

I was in love. Damn! She had forgotten to ask my name. She could have named one little fella Felixitov, after moi. Oh well! Maybe that was quality, but I didn't think so.

The night went on in that vein… a little hunting leading to some mouse casserole. A wee squirmish with a baby rat … I won. I ate him, still wriggling. Chased by a Pit-Bull… all teeth and mucho bark, but no brains and no speed… I won. Or, at least, I didn't lose! I detectified another remote whiff of furrmone from another Queen just beyond my olfartry range. I lost the scent near a bakery… shit!

In short, it was a typical night in the life of a Tomcat. A truly glorious night on the prowl. I was entirely alive.

By dawn, I was pooped and hungry. It had been a stimultifying evening and night. I was ready for milk, a cozy, warm shelf that smelled like me and a huge nap. Hopefully, Fishface and Dakota weren't holding a grunch from that little raccoony thingy. Hell, that thingy cost me half-a-life. What did it cost them? (Only a TV)

I took the fences back home. The Sun was coming up. I paused for another fish meal, in the garbage can… this time minus the raccoon. I ate a gizzard in his memory. Still a lot of good eating in that can. I headed for

our yard. I slowed down to go through the cat-flap.
WHAT? The cat-flap was nailed shut... there was a board
over it with big black letters written across it. No way!
"NO CATS ALOUD!! GET LOST!!" said the sign.

Chapter 4

On the Road Again ... Cat meets Ho

"On the road again...

Goin' places that I've never been.

Seein things that I may never see again...

And I can't wait to get on the road again." —Willie Nelson

My feelings jiltified and my future uncertain, I decided to sleep on it. I hopped up on the heater unit belonging to the She-witch, Fishface's neigboor, who was scared shitless of me. All I did was scratch her a few times and bite her once (TFC). A few wee hisses, now, and she runs like a wuss. She was also a witch. The heater was warm and hummed... like being back in the womb again. I awoke with the vibration of a brick bouncing off the wall above my head. Dakota was tossing bricks and hurling insanities at me. Mostly clichés like, "You f**king cat! Get lost! You maniac cat!" She had her dentures in.   We were no longer close.

I slinkified my way across the yard and down the alley. Dakota had a crappy throwing arm, unlike Fishface, who in retrospecks had proven himself quite ambidexterously brilliant, at that raccoon's expense.

"Zionara to you young Fishface and voluptumous Dakota... you are a pair of losers. This cat is gone from your shallow lives. You had your chance for immorality, and you blew it! Kiss my ass!" I muttered.

I stalkified my way down the alley, my mind made up. I would seek quality and stay alive. On the road again, I set off, heading north.

I refracted on my life... 2 'owners' and 1 ½ lives used up. That left me with 7 1/2 lives to go and the future... what did I want? What did I need?

In fact, I really didn't want an owner... just heat and food and a cosy shelf in the sunshine, maybe a warm human bean to cuddle with and attack once in a while. I truly was a jaguar at heart... but I was also a minisculist at heart. I didn't want much!

One of my favorite programs on TV was 'Eat Your Heart Out, Look at my Manshun!'... which I often watched in the wee hours when Fishface was comatose. It was all about the life of GUPPIES—rich people who lived in manshuns—with 3 garages and lots of fancy silver cars. Owedees, Mersaydees, BMWyas, and Land Rovers. Not a rusty, shit-bucket, F150 Ford pick-up among them. And inside the manshuns they had at least 6 big white crappers and beside the big crappers they had little white crappers to wash their butts off after using the big crappers. So much crap, so little time. And nice carpets all over... lotsa food... and TV's and computers in every room. Rooms and rooms and more rooms.... all decked out with fancy leather sofas and chairs... not one tired Bark-a-lunger. Furniture to climb on and to shred... all the fancy trappings of the Guppy life. All 'Livin the Dream'.

My plan began to germify in my branium: find me a Guppy family, act all nice and cute and cuddly, get myself adopted, and, out to Guppiland I would go. Guppiland was somewhere away from downtown Pittsburg. It had to be, looking at all those trees and bushes, pools, swings, slides and humungus back yards.

Hell... if I played it smart in Guppiland, I could have my own room with a TV with my own remote, gourmay meals, a sundeck to lazify myself on and maybe, maybe my own butler.

"Yessir! Right away, Felix, sir!" Maybe a modest harum of hornified Guppy Queen cats to squirify...

33

I wondered down the sidewalk in a daze, headed for Guppiland. I would find it. I was on a quest. (Like the Man of La Munchies guy!)

"Hey, pussycat, yu wantsa milk?" a voice whispered from a doorway. A stubby Chinesey-looking guy, wearing a bloody apron and a small white cap, smiled at me. He was holding a saucer of milk out toward me. He had a gold tooth top center. "Does the Pope jump rope? Hell Yah! I'm in!" I meowed.

I lapped up the milk while this guy softly strokified my back. I looked around. The sign on the door said 'Ho Chun and Sun, Butchers.' Alright, maybe my move to Guppiland could be defurred for a while. Ho Chun led me into the butcher shop.

A heavenly aroma of raw meat overwhelmed my sensibilities. Ho, by this time, was cuddling me like his firstborn, murmuring lovingly, "Pussy justa time fo suppa. Pussy justa time fo suppa!"

Hell, it was still morning... but, I was game to immerge myself in any new culture that involved me and food.

Ho gently lowered me onto the top of the wooden table that had a delicious smell of fresh meat radiating from it. He gently placed me on my side, stroking my gorgeous coat with his left hand.

I purred. He gave me little tid-bits of pork... mmmm ... pork. Ho had 'new owner' written all across his forehead. He licked his lips. He grinned. I purred like an outboard motor.

Lazily, I looked up.........................to see a mother-fucking cleaver sailing down thru the air toward my neck.

I squirmed and broke his grip... and felt the guillotine blade smacking into the wood, taking a chunk off my good ear. Shit!

I bit him hard in the left hand. Ho needed a lesson in Tomcat hospitality. I wiggled loose and took off for the door.

Howling, "Bans-Eye!...Yahhh!" Ho chased me. Ho was swinging his cleaver like Freddy F. Cougar. I hopped up onto a big pile of pork chops in the window... then leapt to sink my claws into the ass of a big mother-of-glazed-duck hanging down next to the glass. Ho followed me, swinging his gleaming cleaver. The blade kept flashing by my eyes. His gold tooth was flashing in the sunshine.

Giving Ho a target, I did the inverse hanging sloth position (Nature Channel) off the duck, letting my head hang just below the glazed duck's ass.

Ho yelled, "Gotcha sucker!", and took a huge swipe at my branium with the weapon. I ducked. Ho's shimmering steel blade lopped-off the duck's ass ... and, with humungous 'THWACK...IISSCH...' converted his shop window into a few zillion pebbles of glass on the sidewalk. I leaped out through the window to freedom. I meowed, "Gotcha sucker! See ya, Ho!" and sauntered casually down the sidewalk. Then I stopped... Shit! That attack probably constituted yet another life... now 2 ½ and counting. My ear soon stopped bleeding, but it hurt like hell. (15 on the old 1-10 pain score.)

ARTHURS NOTE; Later, I discovered that catmeat remains a delicacy many countries, including large parts of China, Korea, Peru and in the Appalachuns...those hillbilly bastards would eat a shoe if it was dead and had hair. (Animal Planet)

Chapter 5

My Quest for Guppiland And Lives Lost and Found

"Everyone soon or late comes by Rome." —*Robert Browning.*

I hiked the mean streets of Pittsburg all day heading North. I figured that Guppies, being well up the totum pole of life, probably preferred the higher latitudes (the Learning Channel). To tell the truth, I wasn't seeing any manshuns or Mercedees. All I saw were run-down bars and hotels and lotsa garbage, a few rusted-out cars without wheels and quite a few vagrunts with shopping carts.

I decided to look for shiny silver-grey luxury cars ...or at least Whole Foods grocery carts... and then follow the trail backwards, like a trail of breadcrumbs to grandma's house.

I saw a program about Whole Foods on the Bizness Channel. They buy good food and spruce it up... organify it... 'wholify It'... and BINGO, they sell it to the consumer at twice the original price. Maybe it was a scam. Please show me an inorganic vegetable or a cow that does not eat grass or a chicken that is not free to range about their cage. They sell 'Organic' sugar and water... in bottles, with fancy labels... that cost plenty more than gasoline per gallon. And 'cholesterol-free' potato chips. Hell, a potato chip is made from potatoes, vegetable oil and salt. How could the cholesterol sneak into that crunchy treat? And the meat... a pig is a pig is a pig... standing around in its own poop all day. Do Whole Food pigs wear diapers? Same with cows and chickuns. Anyway, Whole Foods was all about good quality food and brilliant marketing. They made Guppies feel good about spending lots of their money while believing they were scarfifying quality ...there's that word again. I loved that Zen guy.

The Guppies I wanted to adopt had to shop at Whole Foods... no Food Lion's folk for this tomcat. NO fake Guppies aloud. Whole Foods was the the key, the Mecca for Guppies. I was on a pilgrummage. Find the Whole Foods and I would my Kaaba Rock (Learning Channel). I walked and walked and walked...

As I headed north it was evening and getting dark. I started to spot more big silver cars, fucking chariots, then even more big sleek silver cars and then huge silver SUB's, all coming out of a humungus parking lot.

A vagrunt on the corner was munching on a sandwich with 'Whole Foods'on the wrapper. A guppy vagrant... a foxy-moron... there is no moron like a foxy-moron.

Guppiland! Whole Foods! The prodrigal son has arrived!

Blazing in the sky above the parking lot across the busy road was the sign, 'WHOLE FOODS'! Like 'HOLLYWOOD,' but way newer and classier. Halleluyah! My body was electrifryed and my stomach lept with joy! So, across the road I skipped, doing a little moon-walk and singing,

"Daddum dada doodum, Doodoo...

Daddum dada doodum, Doo...

Just pick me up fine Guppies

Cause I'm the cat for you."

A squealing of tires on ashfault broke my reverie... A mudderfukkin cement truck's thundering front right tire was inches from my head! I spun, yanking my head away from certain flatitude. I missed being crushed. I flattened my body to the pavement, like an encyclopedia salesman in Bearoot. Half of the 18 or so wheels on that monster truck rolled over my tail... KATHUMP,

KATHUMP, KATHUMP ...My tail... MY Tail.... MY TAIL! Shit!

A cat's tail has 24 bones. My tail bones had just been blendifyed into ONE ... long... long.... very flat one. Shit! My tail was a 1/8 inch thin pancake! (a fucking long skinny flat crepe)

Well, I was alive.

"The purpose of life is to stay alive". (Michael Creighton).

Pissed, I looked up from the cool ashfault ... to see a Felixcidified MANIAC in a Ford F150 shitbox, gunning his motor, bearing down on me... trying to hit me! Was it Fishace? It didn't matter! It was fight or flight.

With a spinning leap, I salvaged what was left of me... to fly off the road. Leaping, I soared through the air and onto the grass, right next to the sign, 'WHOLE FOODS'. I was trembling and sweating in the cool autumn air. I think I had a panic attack.

My age had just transmorphifyed itself... from 2 ½ to fucking 4 1/2 years ... 2 more lives wasted! In one foul swoop. While I was moonwalking to Guppiland I had become middle-aged. Shit!

Was I really nothing but a fool; another pathetic moron? Was I really swimming in the same taintified jeanetic pool where Fishface bathed? Please God, no!

I reminded myself; "Felix, you are a genius... an unlucky genius... a middle-aged, unlucky, mother-fucking genius." And my tail was flat. And my ears were shot. And I was hungry. But I was alive.

I looked at the parking lot; the damn thing was almost empty. The lights in the store flickered, then went off. The SIGN went black.

Someone had closed Whole Foods on me, and the Guppies had all gone home without me! The bastards.

Was it Fishface? No, I was getting a para-noids. Maybe I had caught PSFTD from Fishface, my old genesis. He was not smart enuf to follow me way all the out here to Guppiland. He was too stunned. Fishface was dead to me.

Exhaustified, shaken and hurting, I wandered around to the rear of Whole Foods. The garbage dump-sters were brimming with food. My exquisite scents of smell lead me on a tour, like old Wiley Wonka at the Chocolate Factory. I leapt into the dumpster and explored like I was old Vasco de Gama finding Chinese and Indian food.

Chicken gizzards...fresh. Pork livers and kid-neys ... fragrunt. Fish, fish and more fish, a whole fleet of them: Salmon, swordfish, halibut and cod (no fish stix), all fragrunt and delicious. And cheese: old Cheddar and Budda (not the guy who ate the canary), Stilton, and Camemburp ... wonderful cheese. I georged myself like a

Prince at a feast with NO other cats... just a couple of elderly rats, who I scared shitless.

Maybe I was wrong about 'WHOLE FOODS'. Hell, I was in their dumpster... so this food had to be their 3/4 FOOD or they wouldn't have tossed it. Man, I had just enjoyed a smorgansburg ... a feast. I ate like Hannibal Letcher.

Exhaustifyed after my gourmey meal, I found a nice warm spot, sheltered beneath an overhang, and sat on the heating unit for the store. In a tranquil daze, I groomifyed myself, except for my flat tail (which was a write-off). I stretched, shook, and licked my strokum. My tail hurt like hell (42 on a 1 to 10 pain scale). I drifted into dreamless slumber. Had I discovered Quality?

Chapter 6

My New Guppy Home...the Fox Chapel Gang

"There is only one day left, always starting over: given to us at dawn and taken away from us at dusk."—Jean-Paul Sartre

I awoke to an overcast, drizzly day. Apart from my tail and my ear, what was left of me felt on top of the world... readifyed for a new adventure and Quality (which was confusing the hell out of me). My tail pain had ebbified from 42 down to 17 on the old pain scale, an objectified way to measure something subjective. (Nature Channel... the Sensorified Nervous System).

Not knowing when my next meal would appear, I opted for a return trip to the ¾ FOOD dumpster which was beaconing me... not 20 meters away (Frenchifried measurement 1 meter = 1.094 yards. The Learning Channel). I figured that the ¾ FOOD was down to maybe 11/16 Food by now. But, it was still 10/10 in my humble opinion, which was the only one that mattered. In the dumpster, the 11/16 FOO was still scrumptious: fish, chicken, lamb, pork... all organic... livers, hearts, guts, and brains. 11/16 FOOD, for the descrimified Tomcat. Once again, I dined like royalty.

Editor's Note ... Felix loves ellipses... he calls them ellipsidoodles. I hate them... but WTF. I also hate mnemonics... which Felix loves... so WTF... he is the author from Hell.

Arthurs' Note... Who is getting paid to edit who? She should pay me... WTF. Felix the Tomcat.

Fortifyed, I checked out the parking lot. It was filling nicely with silvery grey Guppimobiles: the usual OMBL Cars (Owdees, Mercedees, BMWyahs, and Land Rovers.) I love mnemonics... and ellipsidoodles.

Editor's Note: See what I mean. Do U hate mnemonics?... me 2! Mnemonics are now banned from this book. Starting now. WTF.

Arthurs Note to Editor: Mnumonics are NOT banned from this ottobiography... You want to make the rules, write your own damn ottobiography.

Editor's note ... *Readers: Please don't write anything to me! I already have shitload of pure crap on my desk to read. WTF!*

Remember: FelixtheTomcat2022@outlook.com *for hate mail.*

I climbed up the lone tree on the edge of the parking lot to establishify an observation platform, of sorts. Today's battle was all about "suck up to your meal ticket." (Entourage... a great series.)

This was bizness. "Make love ... not war." (John Lennon and Bob Marley, 1973)

While I waited and observed, I reflected on a recent TV program on CNBC , featuring an obnoxious loudmouth, Jimmy Kramier... a crassifyed, bald, bizness typhoon with a bunch of childish noise making gizmos. Buy! Buy! Buy! Buy!... Shit! Anyway, the program was called "Winning at Bizness!" On it, Jimmy showed clips of the most famous bizness typhoons stating their 'pearls of truth' about bizness success. The program was like philosophy for materialistic money-grubbing SOBs.

Of course, all Kramier could say was, "Do what I tell ya to do, ya dummies! Why am I always right?" He didn't wait for the answer. All he cared about were his TV Ratings.

But, there was some quality stuff on that program... "The best thing I did was choose the right heroes." (Warren Buffet)

"Opportunities come infrequently. When it rains gold, put out your bucket, not a thimble." (old Warren Buffet again)

And, of course, that ridiculous Rump guy, who sues everyone, especially his own lawyers and girlfriend was yapping away with his weird prematurely-orange hair whipped up like a chikadee's nest (Nature Channel... Bird Dwellings.)

"It is always good to be underestimated." (Rump) It's OK, Mr. Rump, no one could possibly underestimate you enuf.

"As long as you are going to think, think big!" (also Rump).

"Stay hungry. Stay foolish.' (Steve Jobs)

"Hey, is it ignorance or apathy? I don't know and I don't care." (Jimmy Buffet. Warren's brother in Florida).

Up in the tree, I was ready... truly hungrifyed for change (but full of fish). This Tomcat was motivated, ready to think BIG, born into a perpetual state of foolishness. Suddenly, THEY appeared! The speakers in the parking lot played Mendel's 'Halleluyah Chorus'. MY GUPPIES materialized... shimmering in the Sun's rays. The Sun had miraculushly broken thru the clouds the instant that they stepped out of WHOLE FOODS. The Sun illuminated THEM, walking toward me, their new cat.

"Life is like a box of chocolates." (Forest Gump)

She was tall, slim, athletifyed in a sexy way: long Nordick white-blonde hair, and stunning, in her late 30's. She was all decked out in a silky-looking mauve training outfit with a matching sweatband and perfect make-up, right off the front cover of Vague Magazine... a blonde Kate Moss. She held a cell phone up to each of her elegrunt ears, talking and listening to 2 conversations simultaneously. She was speed-walking to the biggest fuckin silver Mercedees SUB in the Western Hemisphere. My Guppiwoman!

Trailing behind her 25 yard was a boy, about 11 years Old, with a golden mop of shining blond hair flopping in the breeze and dental braces glinting in the sunshine. His bright blue eyes were fixed on his Ipad while his fingers flew across the keypad in a white blur. His earplugs, silver and shiny, gleamed in his ears. He was sporting an XXL burgundy Harvard sweatshirt, full of holes. His baggy jeans hung over untied White Jordan Nikes. He had freckles and a happy face. He stumblefyed his way across the parking lot, lost in his technology. He followed his mother's chatty voice to the gleaming silver Mercedees. He looked nice.

But SHE, the mother, SHE was my Afrodite, my Goddess of beauty, my Goddess of love! I was awed.

25 yards behind The GoldenBoy was a girl, chubby and about 15 years old. She sported spiky short black hair, dark lipstick, and a long black duster coat. She

dragged her feet, following the goddess and the Goldenboy. She shuffled along wearily in black work boots. (Dock Martins, I think)

And behind all three comes this guy... a skinnifyed-lookin black fella, just limping along dragging his left leg, wearing a WHOLE FOODS jacket. He was pushing a Hummer of a grocery cart.

The cart was piled up with groceries, like Mount Everisk, stacked right up to 8 feet high. My Guppies either ate well or they were a family of twenty-two.

The skinny guy was trying to chat up the sullen Gloomhilda, "Ah the sun's out! What a day to be alive!"

She scowled, "Maybe for you!"

With no furthers adieus, I hightailed it over to the action and took a stealthifyed position, just under the front bumper of the black Mercedes (mob car) parked behind Afrodite's shiny silver chariot.

The WHOLE FOOD guy, whose nametag read 'Zeus'. (Now that was crappy Karma... but maybe he could fix the weather?)

Zeus worked diligruntly to load the mountain of groceries, mostly green stuff, into the silver chariot's massive trunk. He left the back door open briefly to say, "Thanks for shoppin at WHOLE FOODS," to the Goddess.

Slick as a lizard, I slipped into the luggage compartment and buried my sleek body into a huge cloth bag full of cool Roman Lettuce. I peeked out. Zeus was pocketing a $20 tip.

Looking at me, Zeuss said, "Nice pussy!"

Afrodite said, "Oh thanks! I work out every day!"

Zeuss slammed the door. Afrodite hit the gas.

I hummed,

"Daddum dada doodum, Doodoo...

Daddum dada doodum, Doo!

Ya picked me, Sweet Afrodite,

Cause I'm the cat for you!"

Hopefully, my fate had been casted in better stones... quality stones.

Was I about to start 'livin the dream' in Guppiville? (Turn the page.)

Editor's Note: Felix, treat the reader like they have a brain.

Felix: Unlike you! WTF.

Editor's Note: Your writing style is Chaos-on-a-Page. WTF.

Felix: Thank you, Editor. That is the nicest thing you have ever said to me.

Chapter 7

Guppy Nirvana... Life in Guppy Heaven (LIGH)

'If you come to a fork in the road, take it.'—Yogi Berra

The vibrations of the car and the constant chatter of Afrodite on her cell phones lulled me to sleep. Afrodite had switched one cell phone over to the Mercedees speaker system and held the other phone up to her mouth like a rapper. When I awoke I had the worst urge to pee... so I hosed down the biggest bag of lettuce to keep it fresh.

I peeped out the back window of the Silver Mercedee. Wow! All around us were rolling green hills with white fences and horses and trees and manshuns with 3 or 4 garages and acres of manicured lawns and shrubs around them. Guppy country surrounded me like a comfy down winter coat. We approached a massive bright green metal two-lane security gate (almost like Heaven) with 'Fox Chapel Hill Gated Community' in fancy gold scripture written across it. All the foxes I knew were Atheists! In the stone guard house that controlled traffic into and out of the community stood two burley guards... with AK-47s. (Now those were atheists.)

The guards had scraggly, black hair, ponytails, tons of nose and lip rings, and full beards. Their security company jackets were black leather with no sleeves. The company logo on their vests read 'Hell's Angels' on the back and front with a weird-looking Skeleton head thingy wearing wings plastered across the back. They ooglified Afrodite quite thoroughly.

The Goddess said, "Wow, security is so much better since we hired you fellas!" They nodded back and one of them said, looking at my face poking outa the grocery bag, "Nice pussy." Afrodite said, "In your fucking dreams, Busta!" and hit the gas. We roared through the gates past a coupla mean lookin Harley Choppers.

Afrodite turned the chariot into a paved laneway stretching through a grove of maples arching over the road. She pulled into a long curved driveway cutting through a spacious lawn and slid to a stop.

Afrodite signed off on both phones, "OK, girls. I gotta run. See you at the gym tomorrow." Her phone buddies wished her undying love and kisses. She speed-dialed another number and said, "Hey Rosa. Would you mind coming out to help with the groceries?"

I peeked out at the manshun. It was a three-storey structure... white stone with quadrouple Doric marble columns (Learning Channel) perched on both sides of a regal two-story front Entry, which was at least 30 feet high and mostly glass. More marble columns outlined the 5 garages which stretched away from the massive house like a train of boxcars. The whole place was surrounded by shrubs and planters and lots of black, wrought iron fences encircling the estate. The place was 'The White House meets Alcatraz'. The driveways and walkways were covered in a dizzifying pattern of orange and pink paving stones.

My Guppies were rich. Possibly mega-rich. (MRGs... Mega-Rich Guppies)

Editors Note.... Felix is doing the mnemonics just to piss me off. WTF.

"Money can't buy you happiness... but poverty sucks." (Felix the Cat)

Soon, Afrodite and Goldenboy and even Gloomhilda, reluctantly, were helping little Rosa... their little Guacamolan four- foot, seven-inch domestic fireplug... slugged the groceries inside. I had vacated the bag of soggy lettuce and climbed into a sac containing 'Bolivian Blended 100% Organic Popcorn'. Gloomhilda picked my bag up to carry into the house.

"Holy Shit, Mom! There's a f**king cat in the grocery bag!" Gloomhilda abruptly dropped the bag on the driveway, further injuring my tender ass and tail. Sprawled on the paving stones, I mewed and purred and licked my flattened tail in a pathetic fashion, looking at the georgeous Afrodite with my most pitiful, sad eyes.

"The poor cat is injured. Look at his tail. Look at his ears. The poor little thing looks abused!" Little did she know! I tried to brighten up a bit when she bent over to pet me, I licked her hand and rubbed against her purple silky pant leg... being as much of a suck-up as possible. I deserved an Oscar as leading Tomcat.   Goldenboy piped up, "Mom, you have been promising us more pets for 5 ½ months. Can we keep him? Please!"

Goldenboy was my new BFF. (Best Friend Forever)   "Well, let's take him inside and clean him up and give him some cream and see what Sofia thinks about him." She looked at Gloomer, who now had a bright smile on her face. Afrodite laughed.

Into the mansion we went. Afrodite, Gloomhilda and Godenboy and me... Rosa was still slugging groceries.

The inside of the house was a monster. Enough rooms for the population of Upper Slobovia, with more room for visiting Lower Slobovian relatives. The kitchen was big enough to play road hockey: all gleaming silver appliances, a huge center island (the size of North Dakota) with 8 stools, a glassed-in eating area for 12, and shiny black marble floors. The downstairs stretched on and on: sitting room, dining room, gathering room, living room, library, study, music room, sunroom, laundry room, maid's quarters and mudroom. Afrodite gave me the whole tour in a most modulated, seductified voice. Clearly, she used to sell real estate... or something. The two kids followed us around, both eager to close the deal.

"OK, Elmo, we need you to meet Sofia!" she whispered in my ear ... Elmo? WTF! Sofia? WTF!

Arthurs note: Broke the mnemonics rule. WTF.

On top of one of the 9 sofas on the ground floor sat a middle-age, neutered, (you can tell from the furrmones, or lack there- of) frumpy-looking , porky, white cat. Sofia hissed at me. Afrodite gently lifted her down to the floor beside me. I approached her very timid-ly, wagging my tail and purring. I slowly edged my snout up to her ear and whispered, in Catonese. (the Universal cat language.)

"Sofia, BITCH! You are the number 2 cat in this house starting right now! AND you better act like you love me, or I will fucking destroy your chubby ass and eat your eyeballs!" I explained.

Sofia blinked. She gave me a lackluster lick on my cheek. Her eyes said, "Gangsta!" To simple human beans, hopeless at non- verbal communication, it was love at first sight!

Goldenboy carted me off to the kitchen, lovingly stroking my gorgeous coat in a gentle way, and fed me a big bowl of cream and organic Cat-Bites which tasted vaguely like dead rat. But, hey! I like eating rattus rattus. (Natural channel generic name for the Common Black Rat). I pictured myself being a huge hit in Guppiland.

After the snack, Goldenboy took me upstairs into his bedroom, which was the size of a 7/11 Store. He had his own bathroom and bedroom plus his hobby room. The hobby room contained his collection of exotic animal species in elaborate secure tanks and enclosures. The collection was awesome: a 7 foot yellow, orange and brown patterned boa constrictor called Bo, 4 tarantula spiders (T1-T4), 30 or 40 salt-water fish (Salties) swimming in loops, a dozen foot-long iguanas and lizards, and a pair of parakeets (called Lewis and Quark).

The lime green birds squawked, "Hi handsome!" in unison as we entered the room. Those birds recognized a fine-lookin tomcat when they spotted one.

I found a high shelf to perch on over the room's large windows and watched Goldenboy feed the menagerie. He talked softly to each critter as he worked saying, "The red-tailed boa is a large-bodied snake, up to 13 feet long, living on small rodents. She is primarily found in South and Central America." "Tarantulas are large, hairy arachnids or spiders found in the southwestern US and all of the Southern Hemisphere. Their leg span can be up to 12 inches. They have two extended fangs which can bite and inject venom."

He fed the Boa live mice from a pillow case. Goldenboy would grab a mouse by the tail and lower the squiggling rodent through the top of the cage. The boa lazily lifted its head and… kachug… another mouse went wriggling down the snake's gullet. Note to self… find the motherlode of those cute little white rascals.

Goldenboy softy commented, "The food chain remains alive in the illusion of a natural habitat." That kid was bright, with a big vocabularry.

He fed the tarantulas which crawled up his arms… they were probably de-fanged (Animal Planet). He put dead insects in the cage for the spiders and lizards to eat. Then he spruced up the natural environment, which resembled an Amazon rain forest, complete with warmth and high humidity for Bo the Boa. The parakeets said, "Good job, loverboy!" in unison when the feeding and cleaning was done.

One wall of Goldenboy's bedroom was like a like the bridge of spaceship. Computer screens and keyboards and printers and scanners all hooked up on a cluttered desk covered with books and print-outs and handheld devices. Deftly, he typed in some code and 5 screens lit up with National Geographic photos and boyband music filled the room. The pair of parakeets sang along to Justin Beaver.

Goldenboy cuddled me, "So Elmo, you want to learn about Animals and become computer literate...?" "Hey, pass me the contract!" I mewed back. Little did he know who he was conversifying with.

I licked him, sincerely, on the cheek. It was great to be around someone intelligent, at last. Soon all of the knowledge in the world would be at the mercy of this cat's hyperthymesified memory.

I spent the afternoon napping in the sunroom, a bit dizzified by my spectacular change in fortune. Gloomer arranged a nice bed for me using a quilt off one of the couches. The sunroom would be my home for 'Livin the Dream.' Gloomer seemed to like me too. She kept hugging me and stroking my adorable sleek fur coat.

Sofia had made herself scarce. I caught a glimpse of her napping on the mudroom floor in an old boot. My self-welcoming comments had made an impression on the white wusser. I was happy to glow in my new-found wealth and comfort.

In the early evening I heard a loud engine revving as one of the garage doors opened. I assumed that the king of the castle was home for supper.

Rosa had whipped up a delicious-smelling meal which looked like something from Taco Bell, but better.

When the King walked in through the mudroom from the garage I had the sudden urge to attack him.

His arrival was heralded with an olfartry barrage of girly cologne. He had a mother- fucking red squirrel on top of his head- a dead one. The squirrel had a spikey, orange-red coat and a long tail hanging off the back. He reached up and smoothed the squirrels coat and yelled.

"Honey, I'm home!" He wandered into the kitchen and gave Rosa a pat on the bum and said, "You look happy to see me!"

Rosa scowled, "Usted es un hombre pequeno que es un gran pendejo!" (You are a little man who is a huge asshole... Rosetta's Stones).

A few minutes later the family assembled in the dining room, another room brightified by 10 windows with a 10 foot table and 10 chairs. Rosa served supper. All four members of the family grunted,"Hello", and continued texting, or talking on a cell phone or doing research (Goldenboy) on an iPad. Apart from from Afrodite's shrieks and Giggles, Gloomer's, "No shit! Did she really!"and Goldenboy's, "Aha! So that's how that works!"... supper was free of human interaction. The King stayed constantly on his cell phone, "Well, fucking fire her if she doesn't show tonight!"

Each family member was maroonifyed ... on a separate electronic island. Briefly, I missed Fishface and Dakota yelling curses at each other.

The solitary family discussion centered on the king's statement, "This salad tastes like a cat pissed in it!"

Goldenboy laughed hilariously. Gloomer heaped more salad on her plate and Afrodite just rolled her eyes and looked snarkified. Rosa, lifting her unibrow, snorted with glee and said, "Si, en effecto, un gato hizo la orina en su ensalada." (Yes, indeed, a cat did piss in your salad... Rosetta's Stones.)

Rosa chuckled, and added, "Si, mear. Pero orina fresca en tu ensalada." (Yes, piss. But fresh piss in your salad"... Rosetta's Stone)

Did I have a comrade in the struggle to constantly agitate the guano of life? (mierda de vida.... Rosetta's stones) Rosa could be an ally in my anarchy.

Halfway through supper, the jaguar was growling inside me. I had an overwhelming urge to attack that fucking dead red squirrel on the King's bean. With superfeline effort, I tamed the jaguar inside me. I was trying to appear nice- a Canadian adjective that had never been used in the same sentence with TFC before.

I realized that the other members of the family simply accepted the dead squirrel look as normal. The idiotic squirrel-tail/ ponytail bounced around on the back of his grey-blue golf shirt as he screamed orders into the cell phone while stuffing his mouth with tacos and beans and corn. The shirt had a royal-blue, embroidered badge on the front which read 'STARSTUDS... COFFEE and MORE!" and "Woodrow (Stud) Woodbridge, Boss Man."

I immediately disliked the King. An over-whelming stench of something bold and spicy travelled with him and filled every nook and granny of every room he was in. He was short (maybe five-foot- two) and paunchy and barked orders to some poor sucker on the phone like a Pitbull on testosteroids. He had a jaunty little goatey thing on his face... jet black. He had big white daz-zling capped teeth. The kids ignored him. Afrodite looked at him like a rattus rattus who had just crawled out of a hole in the baseboard.

I had a perfect vantage point to attack the fucking dead red squirrel. I was high up on a buffet above the king's bean...

My patience prevailed. I quieted the inner jaguar... down boy, down boy! The red squirrel and the King could wait. I had to impress the Guppies that I was good and civilized cat ... no gratisfying violence aloud yet.

Later that evening, when all the troops were asleep, I visited the king's room, which was separate from Afrodite's room. On the dresser beside the bed lay the dead red squirrel. In the bed, snoring loudly, was the king, as bald as an eagle. He had a strip of Velcro fastened to his scalp right down the middle of his shining chrome-dome. His name was no longer 'the King'. He was 'Velcrodome'.

As I fell asleep in my bed in the sunroom I had an unusual thought. I was proud of myself. Proud that I had wormed my way into Guppidom (dysfuctional

Guppidom) and I was proud that for once in my 4 ½ lives I had suppressed my inner jaguar, my dark altered- ego. Was this Quality? … god only knew.

Chapter 8

The Digital Cat: Basil goes High-Tech

'The towels were so thick there I could hardly close my suitcase." — Yogi Berra.

The sound of a revving motor and the garage door opening awoke me. That would have been Velcrodome, off to Starstuds and More.

The sun was just popping up over the lovely fields and forest behind the manshun. Sultry rays of sunshine warmed my fur. I had my own private sunroom with a TV and a remote and a computer... and a catflap. The catflap was, no doubt, for Sofia who was clearly a wuss-puss. No outdoor adventures for that chubster. She was afraid to show herself anywhere but the mudroom.

She knew a downtown Pittsburg Tomcat when she was threatened by one. Shit, here in Guppiland, I was the Alpha male.

I had slipped outside through the catflap for a natural interlube a few times, but had not explored much. As a reforming Tomcat, I figured that I better get the lease signed before getting too familiar with the neighboors.

So far in Guppiland, things were looking mighty favorable… I had freedom to roam the house and property, four distracted humans who fed me Whole Food, and kept me warm. No 'owner' was likely to step forward. I could sleep safely, all I wanted. Grooming… hell, my Guppies had 6 bathrooms that I had found. My other needs…to stalk, hunt and kill… to be continued. And regular sex… to be pursued. And open countryside… eat your heart out Willie Nelson! (EYHOWN) I had it made in the shade.

I wandered up to the Goldenboy's room. He was asleep. I cuddled in beside him and he stroked my back and ears and mumbled, "Elmo's a good cat," before falling back to sleep. Goldenboy was a definite "Yes for Felix". He had bought the whole package!

A while later the Goldenboy suddenly sat up and said, "I've got it! I understand the Heisenberg Uncertainty Principle! Hear that Elmo?" He rushed over to the computer and typed in 'Google'. The screen changed and he typed in 'Khan Academy + Quantum Physics.' The screen filled with 'Quantum Physics ' and 'Table of Contents'. He moved a mousy-looking black thing around on a soft pad and clicked it on 'Start Tutorial.'

For the next thirty minutes I watched the Goldenboy control the computer by moving and clicking the mousy-thing. The content of the lesson on Quantum Physics was Greek to me, but his computer beat The Learning Channel by a mile. You could learn what you wanted when you wanted to learn it. I was stupefied.

I went back down to the sunroom (which appeared to be mine) to have a look at the computer gizmos at my disposal. Without much fuss I flipped on the monitor and booted the hard-driver to life. (Goldenboy lesson #1). I gave the mousy-thing pokes with my Paws, manoovering it around, like a baby rat, and clicking it when I hit the right spots. Thank God I wasn't illiterate like most cats.

In seconds I was Googling my brains out. I looked up cat intelligence on Wiki. Wiki was dead wrong. "Cats have the intelligence of 2 year-olds". PULLEASE Louise! I looked up the percentage of unsprayed female cats in suburban Pittsburg... a sorry tale indeed. However...note... unsprayed females tend to cluster in trailer parks and low-income housing estates.

I googled PTFDS and realized that I had probably put Fishface into a state of perceptual retrogression. Pity!

I looked up the inorganic content of potato chips. I was right. No fucking cholesterol was possible! I looked up 100% Blended Oreganic Bolivian Popcorn. It was made by Fritos in Detroit. Whole Foods... you are rascals!

Several hours later, my IQ bulging to new highs, I wandered into the kitchen for a snack: cream and delicious Premium Fresh Fish Fillets- organic cat food (with no guts)- the can said. Rosa beamed her approval in my direction. She probably noticed me stalking the red squirrel on Velcrodome's bean the previous evening. "The enemy of my enemy... yada...yada...yada." (the G).

Afrodite zipped through the kitchen on her way to the gym, looking buff enough to skip all exercise for infinity... but she looked keen to work-out. She gave me a big hug and scratched my neck. I was still in luv.

She grabbed a piece of organic Multigraine Ukeranian flatbread with a smear of humus and an alfalfa/wheatgerms/ parsley smoothie for the road. Yuk. Rosa waited on her like a slave.

Gloomer remained bedbound for the AM. I returned to the sunroom for a serious mid-day naperonie. If this was not heaven someone was playing a nasty joke.

I awoke from my nap sensing the presence of a chubby white cat in my space, hissing and spitting. It was Sofia, ready to boot me out! I faked a look of fear...

mewing and trembled a bit. She looked pleased and hissed a bit more and bared her choppers.

I got up slowly, and ambled over to her. I bit her on the nose and pummeled her 20 or thirty times about the eyes and ears with my paws, leaving vicious scratches all over her head. Oprah meets Muhammud Ali.

She peed herself and then high-tailed it for the mudroom, leaving a trail of urine and blood in her wake. Problemo solved.

Rosa stalked in... "Gato de mierda... Es un imposter!" (You fucking cat... You are an imposter! Rosetta's Stones.)

Rosa cast me a filthy look and proceeded to clean up the mess. I nipped outside for a breath of cool, country air.

In the afternoon I went up to Gloomer's room and scratched on her door. She immediately picked me up and hugged me, kissing me on the neck and nuzzling me with her nose. She looked pretty normal today, no dark lipstick or grungy clothes. She and her friend, Lucy, who apparently was a school friend, were listening to music, dancing and chatting about boys and teachers... the usual stuff. Every few minutes one of them would pick me up to cuddle me. "Oh, Elmo. You are so cute with that flat tail and little chunks out of your ears." I would have preferred that they focus on my strengths! But, I must admit, all the luv felt pretty good. Gloomer, whose real name was Hope, was definitely a "Yes for Felix".

After a while I wandered down the hall to Goldenboy's room. He was just heading down the stairs. I followed him down to the basement which was the size of the New York Subway System. There was a sign... Mouse Farm. Do Not Disturb. Inside, the Goldenboy had a mouse ranch with a huge 4 foot cube of a cage with a wire top. He undid the wire securing a smallish flap on the side of the cage. He reached in and grabbed a mouse by the tail... holding the little bugger upside down so the rodent couldn't bite him.

"Are you afraid of him, Elmo?" I looked the Goldenboy in the eye with bravado and licked my lips and wagged what was left of my tail. He dropped the mouse on the floor. My heart leapt with joy. For the next 10 minutes I stalked and postured and pounced and chased and pounced and bit and chewed that mouse... till I stood at Goldenboy's feet with the mouse carcass in my jaws. Goldenboy was writing down observations in his Ipad. All he said was, "The vertebrate food-chain in action. Good boy, Elmo."

Then he scooped 5 or 6 mice into a pillow case to take up to feed to Bo the Boa. We had a great afternoon: feeding the Boa the wriggling mice, and feeding the spiders and lizards dead bugs from the swimming pool basket and the bug zapper. The fish were boring... but bought back sweet memories of the 11/16 FOODS dumpster. The pair of parakeets were fun… singing Justin Beaver songs.

Later in the afternoon I returned to the sunroom to do a bit more Googling, trying to find a trailer park. Then I met some online cat called Siri who sounded sexy and could speak basic Catonese.

Finally, it was nap time. I needed to rest up. I was eager to head outside for a night on the Guppy countryside… my go-nads needed me to find a trailer park.

Chapter 9

A Night on the Country-side... Felix Makes a Friend

'You and I are more than friends... we're like a really small gang.'—TFC

The moon was well up in the sky when I slippified my way out through the cat-flap. The back yard contained a huge pool, a hot tub, a trampoline, a gazebro and an outdoor kitchen with a BarbBQ and another eating area. My yuppies had about 150 options as to where to park their butts, yet they seldom seemed to sit down.

The expansive lawns stretched off over a meadow toward the edge of a large hardwood bush. In the lawn, there were lots of voles... who are the blind, ugly, mentally-challenged cousins of mice and rats. They were tasty little buggers... I will give them that. But a vole was no challenge to a mouser like Felix the Tomcat.

There was a good collection of Garter snakes (slimy) and lightening bugs (crunchy). Also lots of grass-hoppers (bitter) and BIRDS, a gazillion birds, all over. Birds, chattering and singing, like a symphonified orchistra to this city-boy's ears. Birds moved far too fast for me to catch easily.   I wandered over to the edge of the woods....

There, sitting in the crotch of a big maple was a big, ruff- looking tomcat. He had a brown and black coat with black feet. His ears were mangled, like mine. He had half a tail... and his face said, 'You can call me Mister, mister'. He had bright, intelligent, yellow eyes.

I nodded at him and showed off a bit, chasing a salamander around on the ground and up a tree where it escaped.

"Son, you know those things taste like shit!" he said. He had a deep, melodified voice.

He suddenly pounced 8 feet through the air and snatched a sparrow off a branch with his jaws... and landed softly beside me.

He said, "Here, try this. This is eating!" He dropped the sparrow at my feet.

Nervously, I crunched through the flopping sparrow's branium, and gave the bird a hard shake, till the head fell off. I swallowed the head whole in one gulp.

"Tasty!" I said, choking. I was hoping the cat, who looked plenty tuff, wasn't about to maul me. I wanted to choose my battles after that racoony thing.

"New around here, son?" he asked.

"Yeah, living in the house over there." I pointed at the manshun shimmering white in the starlight.

"How about you?"I asked in Catonese.

He laughed, "Naw, I been here since I was knee-high to a wiener-dog. I live down in the trailer park… with Hank. He drives a truck part-time." Trailer park? Did he say trailer park? I tried to stay cool.

"Hmm! Any other cats living down that way? Any other…um… Tomcats, you know, to hang out with?" I asked, politely.

"Hell no! Well, a couple of old Toms who can't get the flag to half-mast. But you want Queens, Queens in heat, it's pussy galore down at the trailer park."

He continued, "Shit! I'm looking for an assistant to help me with the workload. It's brutal! I came over here tonight to relax. I needed a break!" He suddenly looked tired

I shrugged, "I'd be willing to, um, help ease your burden."

He thought for a few minutes, nodding his dark head.

He said, "Now … don't be telling me you're gay!"

I crossed my heart with my paws, "Straight as a fucking arrow."

He chuckled. "I'm Slick," he said and held up a paw.

"Hey, I'm Felix." I replied, lifting up my paw.

We high-fived… like brothers.

And so began a beautiful friendship, my first and best. Not wanting to push the Queens-in-heat angle right away, I said, "Hey Slick. Show me how to stalk and catch a bird in the bush. I'm from downtown Pittsburg. The birds there were mostly dead."

Slick was amazing. He showed me how to move through the carpet of leaves silently and how to use shadows. He suggested climbing trees on the side opposite your prey. We discussed how to calculate a leap to get the bird, without falling 20 feet to the ground… ouch! He was a regular Grizzly Adams… a Google Search of practical hunting and survival skills. We caught and ate: mice, a load of birds, a chipmunk, a large nasty rattus rattus and a baby squirrel (grey… not red). We had a blast team-chasing a confused hound dog who was lost after a coon hunt. The hours of the night flew by.

As the moon dropped in the sky Slick asked, "Want to see where I live? I'm going to head home for some shut-eye."

He lead me through the bush, uphill and downhill, hopping over streams, and cutting thru meadows… for quite a while. I could hear a highway and a factory nearby. He pointed through the trees.

"There's Hank's trailer… right at the edge of the Slumber Safe Trailer Park."

We sauntered down to the road. Scores of old metal trailers stretched out along a grid of gravel streets toward the highway …dimly lit with the odd streetlamp. There were lots of old junker cars and trucks and washing hanging on clotheslines. Old car parts and cast-off plastic toys were littered across the tiny lawns. Lots of folding lawnchairs, burnt-out campfires, and beer bottles were everywhere. I looked for Fishface to drive in with the old F150… but he didn't show. It was like downtown Pittsburg in the middle of a forest. I briefly suffered a wave of nostalgified memories.

Then, the scent of furrmones hit me smack in the snout. My go-nads immediately responded to the smell of a Queen in heat. Slick poked me in the junk with his paw.

"Wow, son! You may be the Tomcat this job calls for." Before I could find the Queen she found me. A big tabby-cat, her ears twitching, her back arched, her fur standing up, shimmied up to me and rubbed her furrmone -scented face against my neck.

I said, "Bon soir, mon amie. Je pense que tu d'adore. Mon petite cutie-chat!"

She purred and rubbed her soft neck against my chin.

She sidled back and forth, rubbing her soft fur against my sleek coat.

"Tu es tres bellisimo. Mon Cherie!" I added.

"Mount me, you whopper!" she said. She was obviously a Burger King kind of Queen. My Frenchifryed approach was working. But, I wasn't there to discuss fast food. I took her advice and shifted my full attention to her lovely hiney which was elevated and twitching in the moonlight. We copulatted like a couple of wildcats until we both lay on the grass gasping for breath. It felt like the weight of the world had been lifted from my go-nads.

Slick was sleeping on top of Hank's trailer by then. I hopped up and joined him and gave him a soft nudge with my snout. Slick woke up and said,

"How did it go, son?"

I just winked and said, "Dynamite!"

He laughed. "Thanks for stepping in. I'm bushed. That Tabetha cat can't be pregnified. Every two months or so she comes back to give it another go. There's at least 10 more just like her." My jaw dropped...

gaspified. I was counting on my fingers and toes. My new best friend Slick was sitting on the motherlode of Queencat and he seemed to want to share it with me, old Felix the Tomcat.

I sniffed my way back to Guppiland using my olfartry sense and my hyperthymesified memory. It had been a glorious night in the countryside and the trailer park. It was a night I would never forget. And, I had made my first Tomcat friend.

I stumbled through the catflap and lapped up some cream, that someone had left out for me, and fell dead asleep in my comfy quilt.

Chapter 10

Starstuds .... Coffee and More

'Every woman should have four pets in her life. A mink in her closet, a jaguar in her garage, a tiger in her bed, and a jackass to pay for it all.' .... Paris Hilton

I was in the middle of a dream. I was being chased by 3 Queens in heat with a jaguar chasing them. I was shaken awake. Duh! This was not supposed to happen in Guppiland heaven. It was Velcrodome shaking me.

"Hey there Puss'in'Boots. Time to go to work." I was a cat. Cats don't work!

V-Dome picked me up and and tucked me under his arm. He Stank of potent boy perfume like a two-dollar whore. My jaguar was still snoozing... and I was still in suck-up mode. Out to the garage we went and into a sleek red Porch 911 convertible. It was the first Porch I had ever seen except on TV, in the Viagra commercial. On the sides and back of the fire-engine red speedster were huge blue crests reading, 'STARSTUDS… COFFEE and MORE'.

The crests showed a white King Neptude-looking guy with claws for hands perched in a a royal blue circle, Beneath the crests was written, 'Woodrow (Studley) Woodbridge, CEO, CFO' in deep blue.

He chucked me in the passenger seat and VROOM, VROOM, SCREECH… we were off to work.

He had that ridiculous fucking dead red dead squirrel velcroed to his bean, slightly ascrewed. When he dropped the top of the convertible, the fucking squirrel took off, like it was in flight… tail tossing in the wind and the sides lifting up like a magic carpet. Velcrodome was wearing a serious dose of something nasty and strong.

Immediately he fired up the Bluetooth cell Porch phone and started yelling, "Hey, Pittsburg #6. Mr.WoodBridge calling. Get me Belinda." And then, "Did you fire those lazy bastards I told you fire?" and "Good. You know, in spite of your cute little ass, you are a good manager. Keep the bucks rollin' in. Bye. Call me Stud."

"Hey, Pittsburg #12. Mr. WoodBridge calling. Get me Dottie." Then, "Hey Dottie. Did you get that second "MORE ROOM" finished and open? Good. Call my cell at the end of the day with cash flow numbers. And push the 'I got More at Starstuds' hats, teeshirts and mugs will ya!" and "Good. And make sure you're horny when I come down over to Philly next week. Call me Stud."

Velcrodome was driving so fast down the interstate, I thought the fucking squirrel was going to make a sonic boom. (The Learning Channel)

A few minutes later, V-Dome downshifted, hung up the cell and did a half dozen sharp turns through a housing development … we were close to Pittsburg. I could smell factory and exhaust smoke and the traffic was densified. He screeched to a halt in the alley behind a strip mall opposite a huge suburban high school. Just down the road we had driven by a large community college. V-Dome yapped incessibly.

"Great location, Boots. This store is going to make me a lot of money. This will be store number 57… from Newark, New Jersey to Philly and Pittsburg and all the way up to Boston, Mass!" My antimousity toward this turkey was growing, like a fungus.

V-dome and me waddled into the Starbuds through the back door. Outside the front door in a large parking lot a huge crowd had gathered, all waiting for the brand new store to open at 8 AM. Teenagers from the high school and college, truckers, teachers, fireman, cops and regular folks joined the crowd… all curious to see the new store. They milled about, talking and looking in the windows.

The front of the store was like a Starbucks but more spacious... maybe 30 seats and a counter. The place was spotless... tile floors and polished tables. Fine art prints of sailboats filled walls. The display case showed a mix of treats: pastries, donuts, bagels, salads, sandwiches. All the stuff looked fresh. Being an obligated carnivore, I was not tempted. The staff were friendly. They were all female, young and pretty and they all smiled nervously at V- dome as he duckwalked, regally, through the store and up to the counter.

The manager, Michaela, was a beautiful, slim Hispanic woman with big mammary glands and warm smile. She blushed when she saw V- Dome and gave him a hug. "Oh, Meester WoodBridge, I am so excited. Day one! Look at the crowd." She did a little Cuckaracha dance.

V-dome smiled, puffing up his chest like a ruffled grouse, and spoke to the assembled store workers,

"I expect this store, Starbuds #57, to be exceptional. Michaela and I will treat all of you well, but we expect loyalty, honesty and hard work in return for $1 more per hour than the Starbucks down the street."

The staff, all pumped, busted into song:

"We love Starstuds... Ya, Ya , Ya," to the tune of 'She Loves You,' by the Beatles.

V-Dome gave the staff a fist bumps and pats on the bum and turned to Michaela, "Now, show me the More Rooms."

She smiled, "Yes, boss."

I followed them to the back half of the store. Michaela showed us the men's and women's washrooms which were huge, tiled and clean. Between the two washrooms were two "MORE ROOMS'.

Michaela slid her manager's card into an electronic credit card reader on the door to 'MORE ROOM #1'. A white sign read, '$10 for 10 minutes… CHANGE YOUR BABY!' V-Dome grinned a letchurly smile.

The door clicked open, the signed turned green and she giggled and stepped into the room. The door clicked closed. The green light above the door started flashing amber. V-dome whipped his owner's card through the reader and stepped through the door to follow Michaela. I scooted in on his heels. The light inside (and outside) the room flashed purple… and the sign above the light flashed 'GETTING MORE at STARSTUDS!'

The MORE ROOM was small and simple. The room had tile on the walls and floor, piped in jazz music, with a single 3'x 6' bed at the height of a change table. A sign on the wall said, 'Change your babies here."

Doors led out of the back of the More Room with arrows pointing right to 'Mens' and left to 'Women', leading back to the washrooms. Clean sheets and towels filled a small cabinet in the corner. V-dome had his arms around Michaela and was nuzzling her neck when he noticed me. "Get out Boots- this place is for horny people, not cats." I was helped out of the room by V-Dome's shoe on my butt.

Eight minutes later Michaela and V-Dome emerged from their respective washrooms… grinning. V-Domes red squirrel had shifted 45 degrees. He was starting to look like Davey Crockett in his coon-skin hat.

V-Dome stood up on a chair and said, 'Beautiful ladies, start your engines!" Michaela opened the door and the throng flooded in at 8 AM o'clock sharp.

The sign above the coffee counter said,

"COFFEE medium… $2.00. Pastries and Sandwiches… Half price!'

The crowd lined up at the counter three deep, smiling and chatting, sipping coffee and scarfifying pastries. Michaela encouraged people to the extra outside seating to ease the crowd.

Both the 'MORE ROOMS' had long lineups of giggling couples, young and old, gay and straight.

People, most often a man and a woman, a minute or so apart, slid their credit cards into the machine which read, '$10 for 10 minutes'. The door clicked open …

the second person put in their charge card… and followed. The door clicked shut.

Over and over, the signs over the rooms flashed purple, "GETTING MORE at STARSTUDS'. About 10 minutes later, the same two people would exit, from the men's or women's washrooms… separately… looking flushed with slightly embarrassed smirks on their faces.

The light over the door flashed white again, 'Ready FOR MORE'. 'CHANGE YOUR BABY'. Smiling, paying customers stepped into the 'MORE ROOMS'. Do the math….

Outside the store, in the parking lot, the students, high school and college, were howling and back-slapping as their pals emerged from the Starstuds, with coffee, food, and, almost always, an 'I GOT MORE AT STARSTUDS' hat or teeshirt. Everyone was having a blast.

V-dome was giving a motivational talk to all the employees as they worked in his CEO, CFO voice. All the while, he was rubbing Michaela's back behind the counter. She did not seem to mind.

After a few hours the store's business remained brisk, even after the students stumbled off to school.

Velcro and I hit the road, popping into 7 more stores all around the perimeter and downtown portions of Pittsburg. The business model worked like magic. Some of the stores were near mall, where working people in business suits hooked up with sales people stopping for coffee and more. The university campus store was packed with students, talking and drinking coffee, eating lunch and having quickies. Teeshirts and hats were flying off the shelves. A few stores, near factories, overflowed with workers and, sometimes, hot-looking women with short skirts.

Eventually, V-dome swung by the manshun and tossed me out on the driveway. "See ya, Boots!" he said as the Porch 911 laid rubber down the gracefully curved lane.

V-Dome was an asshole... an asshole who was two-timing the woman I loved. But what could I say? I was a Tomcat too.

I snuck into the manshun through the cat-flap. The house was quiet except for Rosa who was busy dusting in one of the sitting rooms.

I approached her... mewing and rubbing my fur against her stubby legs. She whacked me on the head with her dust mop,

"Maldito loco gato! Maldito loco gato!" (You fucking maniac cat!... Rosetta's Stones)

But I was whipped and I had to see my new friend and I had to fufill my challenging new role as Slick's surrocat. I had some serious con-sexual koitus to engage in... in a few short hours. This Tomcat needed shuteye.

Chapter 11

Attacked... Another Life Bites the Dirt

"There are worse things in life than death. Have you spent ever spent an evening with an insurance salesman?" Woody Allen

When I awoke, the family was sitting in the dining room eating Pizza. Sofia was nowhere to be found. Afrodite, the Goldenboy and Gloomer all looked up from their iPads to smile at me. They passed me around. Afrodite smelled like some heavenly blend of caramel and sandalwood. We cats are superiorfied when it comes to olfartry senses. V-Dome was home, yapping into his phone and shovelling pizza into his piehole like a ditch-digger on meth. Rosa brought him more pizza and commented,

"Pequeno hombrecita detestable. Estas gordo porque comes como un cerdo." (You obnoxious little man. You are fat because you are eating like a swine. Rosetta's Stones.)   Gloomer almost fell off her chair laughing. She was studying Spanish in Tenth Grade. I could not suppress a little giggle myself. V- Dome looked temporarily confused and started scarfifying a big piece of the Meat-Lovers special thick Cheese Crust pizza. He was drinking rum and coke.

Afrodite picked away at a kale, and cherry tomato salad. Every once in a while she would squeeze the skin of her shapely butt with two fingers, checking for fat, beneath the tight fabric of her electric pink tights. If you could find three ounces of fat on that body you could sell it on E-Bay as a rare collectible! She was as keen on exercise as much as V-Dome hated it. He wore his usual outfit... blue Starstuds golf shirt with "The Boss... Call me Stud" embroidified below the Starstuds emblum. Rosa tossed a cherry pie and ice cream on the table and sniped,

"Comer gordo. Tus coronarias se Tagaran esto." (Eat up Fatboy. Your coronaries will gobble this up." Rosetta's Stones.)

Goldenboy and Gloomer and V-Dome all enjoyed a fat slice of pie and a cupla scoops of ice-cream. I licked out Goldenboy's bowl with my Velcro-like tongue when he was done. The family was falling under my spell. Afrodite retired to the exercise bike and V-Dome had a snooze on one of the 12 couches.

It was getting dark as I wandered through my catflap for another night on the prowl. Life was good. Lots of food. My rest was free from predators, except Sofia (see the next chapter) and intermittently, that miniature Spanish attack dog, Rosa.

But, I was livin the dream in Guppiland. I crossed the open fields and approached the huge maple at the edge of the woodland. Slick was parked in the notch of the tree, lookin fine. His black-brown coat was freshly preened and he was giving his strokum a good cleaning with his raspy tongue. He grinned,

"Hey kid. Are ya ready for a little action?"

I nodded. "You bet, Slick. You are the Man."

Slick said, "No, You the Man, Brother."

We banterfied back and forth a few minutes on who, in fact, was the Man. I was standing in the meadow below the tree with the moonlight illuminating my jaguaresque fur.

Suddenly, there was a loud "SCREECH, SCREECH, SCREECH" and realized I was being lifted by a giant set of claws as sharp 2-inch long talons bit into both sides of my back. The loud, flpping sound of a 5 foot wide wingspan, beating to create lift, pierced the quiet night.

"SCREECH, SCREECH, SCREECH!" Screamed the huge raptor.

I rotated my neck 180 degrees to correctly visualize my abductifyer. It was a GREAT HORNIFIED fucking OWL (Bubo virginianus... Animal Planet) That Owl was no virgin. Her face had a sharp hooked beak and her huge yellow eyes stared at me as she swept me off the ground. We climbed higher and she squeezed harder. I wriggled and snapped and bit everything I could. Every bite yielded nothing but feathers! Her talons, three going forward and one backwards, squeezed me with 400 pounds of pressure per square inch.

Oddly, as we approached the top of the tree, 60 feet up in the air, she backed off on the beating wings and started to glide in peaceful loops over the meadow. She was showing off her perfect control over her prey... who was praying, "Dear God. Get me outa this jam and I will be a good Christian or Buddist or Hindu Tomcat... starting now. Praise God!"

When the owl did a victory lap, she swoopified perilously close to the base of the giant maple just to show me that I was truly doomified. That sucker could fly and I was in her death grip.

With a loud hiss and snarl, my loyal Tomcat friend, Slick, cat- a-pulted outa the tree and landed on the owl's back, with his ample jaws and razored teeth sunk into the back of the owls neck. That sucker, Slick, could jump better than a jackrabbit. With Slicks long teeth and strong jaws threatening her spinal cord (Animal Planet) the owl released me and I fell 15 feet to the meadow. My cat-like reflexes ensured that I landed lightly on my paws. I scampered to safety in the crotch of the maple. Slick, tired of chewing on the owl's head, dropped down to safety and joined me in the maple tree.

"And that's why ya never stand out in a meadow in the moonlight near big trees!" said Slick.

I wished he had mentioned that earlier.

I said, "Shit. Slick, I am up to 5 ½ lives, Slick. I just burned another life.

Thank you for the brave rescue. I was toast."

Slick was a true friend. "I get by with a little help from my friends." (The Beatles)

Slick said, "Death is life telling you to slow down."

Slick said he was up to 6 lives lost and he was only a year my senior.

We made a pinky-promise to live smarter, and longer.

The night on the prowl had been sobered a bit by my loss of a life, but we decided to plunge ahead with some hunting and, hopefully, some serious con-sexual koitus. I was nervous in the wide- open, so Slick led me to a grain field where we hunted rodents along the edge of a barbed wire fence. There is no better owl than an owl behind barbed wire.

The grain field was a cat Smorgusburg and an owl jail. I munched down seven field mice (apodermus sylvaticus... Google) and 1 largish rattus rattus (common black rat...Google). I ate only the best, most lively field mice because they carried this virus thingy called Hankyvirus which can cause a Pulmonary Syndome, meaning your lungs get screwified.

I educated Slick, who was not a reader. Slick was illiterafied and not Googlified at all. I suspeculated that hankyvirus got its name from hanky-panky and that Hankivirus infection was part of the STD speculum. STD is Sexually Transmogrified Disease, if you didn't know (Google). I loved Google and spent at least 3 hours a day feeding data to my seriously hyperthymesified branium. Slick and I were an awesome team. Slick had street and forest smarts and I had 'Everything else' smarts.

With full tummies and one badly talon-scarred back we headed to the Slumber Safe Trailer Park. A beat-up F150 truck sat in front of Slick and Hank's trailer. We wandered in through the cat- flap. The place was tired: worn carpet, kinda grubby, a table with two chairs, dirty dishes in the sink, a few beer bottles stroon around, a threadbare sofa and chair. Hank was parked in the chair, drinking coffee and snoozing. He nodded awake and looked at me,

"Hey, another cat," and fell back to sleep. In my life, that qualified as a warm reception. Slick nodded his approval and we went outside to audition some Queens in need.

Editors Note: Sorry, folks... Felix has created his own GDL (Goddammed Language) called English Plus. He claims it's the future of prose ... completely originalified words. Hey (WTF)... I am pretty powerless in dealing with that rogue, Felix (TFC).

Felix: Thankyou for calling me 'a fresh literarified voice'.

My frenchified approach to luv was enthusiastically received by three Queens in estrus: a cute grey cat with sparkling eyes, Zelda, a striped tawny yellow Queen called Florence, and a skinny, but seriously horny black and white Queen called Elizabeth the Second (she claimed royalty in her bloodline.) I called Elizabeth "Your Royal Highness" in French, ("Votre Altesse Royale"... Rosetta's Stones) which turned her into a sexual maniac.

I was whipped. Slick, who was pacing himself restricted his copulation to a pair of twin Queens visiting from Wheeling, West Virginia. (country cats)

Editor's Note: I have been teaching Felix the correct use of the semicolon; which he has now employed as a means to create irrelevant run-on, verbose sentences. Again; WTF, WTF, WTF.

Arthurs comment... Now that; is the pot calling the kettle black.

It was a good night. Slick and I had a nap for a couple Hours under the trailer. Apart from a black snake (which we jointly mauled) we slept, peacefully and restfully, like a coupla kittens.

Slick walked me back to the maple tree; I was nervous of Great Horney Owls; and then I dashed across the meadows to the manshun.

As a last thought before sleeping, I creptified my way upstairs and swiped V-Domes very smelly, red squirrel wig off his dresser. He looked peaceful with star-light reflecting off his Velcrodome as he snorified his way through a night's sleep.

I took the hairpiece down to the mudroom. Sofia, terrified, was not there. She had shifted to hiding mode. I rolled the red squirrel hairpiece in Sofia's crapola in the litter box... and then peed on the resulting log of kitty-litter shit. It was the Yule Log from Hell; Sofia was going to know deep doo-doo. Early in the morning, I was awakened by V-Dome yelling at Rosa.

"Where the fuck did my best hairpiece go? Did you move it off my dresser?"

He was standing in the kitchen with his fat belly popping out between a small tight white t-shirt and a pair of drooping red boxer shorts. Rosa looked at him and said, "No tengo ni puta idea donde esta ese feo trozo de alfombra! Estupido!" ("I have no fucking idea where that ugly piece of fur has gone! Asshole!" Rosetta's stones.)

Velcrodome proceeded to search the place... He checked my sunroom first. I resented the display of mistrust. Then he checked the Gloomer's room... nada.

Then he checked the mudroom. There was a furious scream..." That motherfucking Sofia shit in my wig and rolled it in Kitty-Litter."

Rosa, chuckling, added, "Como un tronco de Navidad del infiero, pendejo!" "Like a Yule Log from Hell, Asshole!" Rosetta's stones.

I had a big saucer of warm cream from Rosa... we were growing on each other. I hit the sack, exhausted from a terrifying and stimulafying night on the prowl. I was up to 5 ½ lives... time to kick back a bit. I was awakened by Afrodite cooking egg whites in the kitchen. Perched on the counter was a metal cage thingy about the size of a weekend suitcase. Inside, looking like John Fucking Gotti, was Sofia who scowled at me and hissed and shook her paw at me. She was insanely pissified.

Afrodite chirped happily, "And don't worry, Sofia honey, you are going to love Uncle Freddie's pig farm. You are going to live in the barn with all the barn cats. It will be like summer camp. It will be fuuun!" Sofia looked ill. As the pair disappeared into the garage to drive the huge silver Mercedees to rural Podunk, Pennsylvania, I heard Sofia puking in her cage.

"Revenge is beneath me. Accidents, however, will happen." Felix the Tomcat.

I fell asleep again until 3 PM when the two kids returned from school. They both were hungry and gave me hugs and peperoni while they scarfified some leftover pizza. I gave them both some licks with my raspy tongue and amplified my most mellow purr. Human beans love that stuff.

Goldenboy invited me up to his bedroom/lab, "Hey, Elmo, come on up to my room. I have an idea for my science project. You are going to be the study object. Hmmm, study object. That sounded intense, but maybe. Goldenboy flipped on the computer and Googled, 'The Science of Cats'. He had not graspified the depth of my intelligence, my reading ability or my memory (yet). Here was my chance to show off my copulous natural gifts.

The U-Tube Video we watched showed this bald skinny guy with perfesser glasses (eat your heart out John Lennon glasses (EHOJL glasses)) testing a rather ordinary lookin brown tabby-cat's reflexes. The perfesser would hit a weenie-button on a remote and a metal tray with a cat-treat would appear then disappear in a flash. That cat would react in a flasheroo to scoop the treat off the tray with its tongue before it disappeared again. The perfesser said, "Cat reflexes (7-20 milliseconds) are 10 to 15 times quicker than human beans (200 millseconds) and 1.5 times faster than dogs. (20-30 milliseconds)." That cat was super quick on the draw.

Next the perfesser cranks the cat on a little shelf way up in the air... 20 feet with a rope contraption on a long verticalized flag- pole (no flag please... they were British).

The cat was standing on a platform, way up in the air, lookin mildly pissed off with the whole adventure. The perfesser poked a red button and the shelf collapsed and the cat fell like an apple (a la Newton) to the pile of matresses on the ground. Of course, the cat righted itself (righting reflux... Animal Planet) in the air and landed purrfectly on its four paws, and then went back to licking his strokum shortly after landing.

Research: Google states that cats can fall up to 200 feet (13 stories) and land safely. This is because the terminalized velocity of a cat is 60 mph versus 120 mph for a human bean. Cats have a large surface area to weight ratio and spread their limbs out while they fall. Maximum velocity is achieved at seven stories. So, for any cats who want to jump/fall... go big or go home. One 'lucky' feline fell 32 stories in New York and survived. (Formally known as Prince, he is now called 'Slim.')

Goldenboy was bubbling with excitement, "Elmo, I am going to build a reflex timing machine and a falling tower and statistically analyze your reaction times. I might even test you against a few other cats. The Pennsylvania Science Project winners this year get to go to Harvard for the East Coast Cup." Whoopdy- doo... a road trip. Maybe a road trip for me and Slick... hmmm.

We went to the basement to bag some mice for Bo the Boa. Goldenboy let me chase, terrorize and eat 2 white mice today. The lab mouse flavour does hot compare to the dilectified flavor of the field mouse, but, at least they don't have Hankyvirus. Goldenboy admired my stealth and pounce technique, muttering, "Ah, the circle of life, the circle of life" like old Mufasa in the 'Lion King.' I love Goldenboy. He is my kinda guy. Anyway, we gathered 8 mice in a bag. (a bag of mice are way more fun than a bag of cats)

The roar of a Porch911 convertible skidding into the quadrupilized garage announced the arrival of V-Dome. Oh my God … he was wearing a new hairpiece. It was a furry, sandy brown thing with the hair standing straight up and extended from just above his heavy black eyebrows to the back of his neck. It had to be a dead beaver (made in Canada). The fucking thing looked like the loser of a beaver meets a NASA Wind-tunnel matchup.

He looked at Afrodite and asked, "Do you like it?"

She said, "Like what?" ignoring him.

Rosa muttered, "Parece un puto castor muorto, pendejo!" (It looks like a dead fucking beaver, asshole. Rosetta's Stones.)

Gloomer literally fell off her kitchen stool laughing. She loved taking Spanish at school. Rosa belonged on Comedy Centrified.

Editors Note: Unless this is a best selling memoire, I quit.

Arthurs Note: … go ahead… WTF.

Chapter 12

Another Night Prowlifying
with Slick

I was greatly enjoying being the Cat prince of the manshun with Sofia's move to swine heaven. Rosa was growing on me, even though she saw through me like a cheap suit. With the help of Rosetta's Stones, I loved her nastified barbs aimed at Velcro-Dome. He paid her weekly in 20$ bills, which I expect came directly from a Starstud's cash drawer. He offered an advanced weekend course in 'Cash Capture' (skimming) to his store managers who showed Initiative. For each $100 they could divert as cash to him with no record he gave them $20 bonus. They were delighted.

I concludified that Rosa was an illegal immigrunt and that Velcro-Dome was probably breaking at least 10 statues regarding the hiring of illegal

Guacamolans. So, I had leverage on both Rosa , who I liked, and Velcro-Dome, who I detestified. To quote Yogi Berra, "You can observe a lot by watching."

I headed out the cat flap at about 9 PM. I was watching re- runs of 'House' to brush up on my medical knowledge. House was pretty smart at diagnosifying rare and mortifying diseases. I suspected he had a hyperthymesified memory, like me. Tonight he was solving a case of Glioma tumor in the frontfied lobe of the branium that caused a 42-year-old preacher lady to become a compulsified gambler. He bet her $100 bucks that he could diagnosify her in less than a week and cleaned up like a street-sweeper. Of course, he operated and removed the offensive mass to save her life. She celebrated with a week in Vegas.

"The key to success is not through achievement but through enthusiasm." Malcolm Forbes

Slick was waiting in the maple tree, snacking on sparrows that were out looking for bugs to eat.

"Ask not what you can do for your country. Ask what's for lunch." (Orson Wells).

Slick gave me a few more tips on having bird lunch vs. being bird lunch. (AKA the Great Hornified Owl). I was getting pretty slick at catching and killing birds; I was becoming Slickified in the Outdoor Survival Arts. (OSA's) I lept out of the maple on a fat Robin which was trying to tuggify a fat juicy worm out of the meadow.

The Robin was downright tasty, but the worm tasted like a shit sandwich.

We ventured over to the grain field and had the buffet special of field mice (healthy ones – forget Hankyvirus at your peril, pussycat) with a porky rattus rattus (black rat) for dessert. Cats are called obligatified carnivores because they must eat meat as a biologic necessity. Yes, your cuddly, furry, pure-white Salamise cat is, indeedy-do, a vicious predator in her heart of hearts. She must eat meat for the aminofied acids in animal protein such as TAURINE- essential for good eyesight, nervous function, the immunization system and the heart. That also explains the four needle-sharp piercing teeth (Canine teeth... What? Yes, Felix, Canine), issued by God (or maybe Satan) to all obligatified carnivores (OCs). In the group of OCs are: all cats... big, small, domestic or wild, jungle or towncats, including lions, tigers, jaguars and me. Carnivores also include Crocodiliams, owls...(ya think?), eagles, vultures, and all canids: dogs, bears, wolves, foxes, and hyenas- with or without go-nads. Finally, the Carnivores include dolphins (Flipper- you rascal), snakes (figures), scorpions, marlins (the fish, not the baseball players), groupers (the fish, not the fools who chase rock groups), and, of course, pirannas (those Africanized guppyfish with nasty choppers), and finally sharks (the fish, not the Hockey team).

Editors note... (EHOJA) Eat your heart out Jane Austin... talk about an illconstructed, ramblified, idiotic, boring, run-on sentence; Felix just wrote the motherfucker of all boring, ill-

constructed, ramblified, idiotified sentences. (TGYPS... there goes your Pullitzer, Sucker) WTF. I quit again.

Arthurs Note: You cannot quit twice. It should read, "I quits."(plural verb) Besides,"You are fired, Bu-Bye!"

Arthur's note: example of a plural verb; "the baby shit his diaper." Vs "The baby shits his diaper every time we feed him corn-on-the-cob."

Slick and I proceeded on to the Slumber Safe Trailer park for some hot, wild con-sexual coitus. Wow... the Queens were in serious estrus aujoir-dwee! I will not give you all the detailed, intimate details. This is not the porn section of the book. (see the sequel). A gentleman Tomcat does not always kiss and tell. Enuf to say that lively con-sexual Koitus was practified, perfectified and enjoyed with vigor by all parties. By the time we were finished my swimmers were doing the back-stroke.

Slick and I flopped out on the trailer roof to nap till the sun was coming up. Hank was up making breakfast; he was driving a load of hay up to Buffalo this morning. He was reading a paper on his iPad, just touching the screen with his finger. Awesome, I needed one of those things. If I could charm one outa Goldenboy, there would be no stopping my computer exploration. My knowledge was already growing in an exponentified fashion.

Slick was street-smart, but Hank was smart-smart. Hank had a big vocubularry and talked real fast about interesting stuff: Does John Kerry really wear a wig? Is Joe Biden's son's art that bad? Is Donald Rump really an alien? (Hank says yes!) Who shot JFK? (Hank says the CIA did it. Really fascinating stuff. And Hank could have a lively discussion with himself. (maybe TMYIATS... Too many years in a Truck Syndrome) Anyway, Hank gave me some cat-treats and a bowl of cream and let me lick his yellowed, nictotiny fingers. We were going to be pals.

Hank said, "Hey fellas... how be you come with me on my next run up to Niagara Falls next week. I am going to visit my looney- toons sister and her husband, who is a Furry." Both Slick and I nodded in unisome. A road trip to Niagara Falls to visit a Furry. What could possibly go wrong?

I wandered home, super aware of Great Horny Owls, and had some cream and some Whole Foods tuna and crashed for a few hours of sleep. Velcrodome wandered through with his new beaver hairpiece gleaming in the morning light. In the back of the hairpiece was a little stub of something shiny and black. I assumed it was the stubby remnant of the beaver's tail.

Gloomer punched Rosa in the arm and said,

"Parace que el castor se esta cagando!" ("Looks like the beaver is taking a poop." Rosetta's Stones.) Rosa howled with laughter.

Goldenboy said, "Damn, I need to study Spanish on Khan Acadaemy."

The quest for knowledge in this house was augmentified by a second language. (right brain, left brain)

Chapter 13

Another Life in Jeperdy

I was rudly awakened from sleep by my sweetheart, Afrodite, who was looking fabulous as normal wearing cowboy boots, blue jeans and a tight pale blue cashmore sweater that featured her ample boobs. She had her chipper voice on,

"Hey, Elmo, we are going on a little adventure today! You have been out all night again, you horny little bugger." She had no idea how much I understood.

I was suspicious. However, I did enjoy her company, even with the constant nattering on several phones simultaneously. She was a multi-taskerite alright. She was talking to Jenny about liposuction and Marguerita about a Woman's March for Colitis and making some sense. She drove the Silver Bullet through the winding country roads at 122 mph with one hand. Her profile was beautiful: perfect arched eyebrows, a smokey look around her gorgeous blue eyes, flowing shoulder-length, naturally-curlified ash-blonde hair, pouty full violet-red lips and sparkling white straight teeth. She was right outa Vague Magazine.

We pulled into a one-story building with a half-full parking lot. The sign said, "Rolling Hills Veterinary Clinic ... Small Animals." Dr. Fred Slumkowski, Veterinary Surgeon.

Wait. What? A vet... for who. Surely not me. I felt great. I looked around the car. Afrodite, bathed in perfection, was not in need of a vet. By my intuitive powers of deductability I concluded that I was probably the patient. I had never seen a vet before and had no urge to launchify down that slippery slope.

Afrodite gently grabbed me and shimmied into the clinic. The reception staff welcomed us and stuck a little name tag on my butt ... 'Elmo Shultz- Castration'!

At that very second a huge man who looked like a Steelers' lineblocker wandered into the room and scooped me up heading for the operating theatre.

"I am Dr. Slumkowski, ma'am, a little 'snip-snip' under anesthesia and he will be a new cat. A quiet, well-behaved citizen cat."

This Dr. Slumkowski guy musta skipped the lecture on 'informified consent'. No 'snip-snip' for this Cat was going to happen- ever. He kept giving me a creepy smile while his assistant handed him stuff to start an intravenous (I watch ER reruns) to put me to sleep. When his hands were both busy, I launchified my attack. "The two most powerful warriors are patience and time." The General "Freedom is never free."

Snarling and spitting I lept up and dug my 10 front claws deeply into his face. Then, I bit his nose and tore a chunk outa both of his ears with my razored teeth. He howled in pain... but being a professional, he could not just toss me like Fishface. He tried to reason with me,

"Hey, little fella, just gonna put you to sleep for a little snip-snip."

"Snip my ass!" I hissed.

I sunk my four canines deep into his penis... right through his scrub pants. I pictured myself in Nathan's Annual Hot-Dog Eating contest and chewed like Joey Chestnut (the habitual winner). The vet screamed like an Elvis fan and fainted. The two nurses also fainted. The official score was Felix 3: Team Slumkowski 0.

I swaggered out of the OR suit with a grin on my face like I just transplantified a coupla hearts. I jumped up on Afrodite's lap. She stroked my gorgeous yellow, white, black and brown, soft, rosettified coat. I purred and turned up the amp.

"Are you OK, sweetie?" she inquired. I gave her hand a reassuring lick and pointed to the car keys with my paws.

She yelled, "Just mail us the bill." to the receptionist and off we went. The dirty deed had been done... just ask Dr. Slumkowski. The nurses were calling an ambulance for him.

That little melee did not count as another life lost. I was still at 5 ½. Dr. Slumkowski... maybe another story. No little Slumkowskis would be swimming out of that guy for a few weeks.

And so, Felix the Tomcat continued on as a go-nadally gifted Feline, even though Velcrodome and Afrodite believed that I had been fixed. Goldenboy figured it out in a flash... I still had junk!

Arthur's Note... when the Vet Bill arrived a week later it read:

Veternary Consultation Fee $250

Time in Surgery Fee $200

Time in Anesthesia fee $150

Traumatized Penis repair $1000

Plastic surgery fee for partially amputated ears (2 @ $1200) = $2400

Plastic Surgery fee for 10 severe lacerations (face and nose) = $4500

Psychiatry consultation for PTFSD $800

Emergency visit and tetanus shot with IV antibiotics $1500

Total cost $10,800 (payable immediately)

PS. Do <u>not</u> bring this animal to this clinic <u>ever again</u>. <u>Please</u>, I beg you,

Sincerely yours,

Dr. Fred Slumkowski, BSc, BVSc.

Velcrodome paid cash and got a $1000 discount. Not only did I win the battle, I won the war.

The family was shocked at how fast I bounced back from my surgery.

Chapter 14

Training for the Sinus Fair

"The past, the present and the future walked into a bar. It was tense."

I slept the afternoon away. The kids got home from school and I joined Rosa and Goldenboy and Gloomer in the kitchen for a bowl of cream and a helping of chicken thighs. (Whole Foods organic grass-fed). I hung out with Gloomer for a bit. She brushed my coat and enjoyed my purring and raspy finger-licking. She was a pushover, but I liked her. She was real. When she got busy texting her friends, I wandered down the hall to see Goldenboy.

"Hey, my research partner, Dr. Elmo, has arrived. This is going to be a killer Sinus Project!" "Kill who?" I wondered, but jumped up on the desk to see his sketches of the apparatchuks for the experiment. For reflex testing he had purchased a 12 inch wide and 3 inch tall thingy in the shape of a circle with 4 bright panelled lights on top... green, blue, yellow and purple. Most cats were red-green colour blind, but, I could easily distinguish those four colour panels, especially when illumified. Goldenboy had this gadget wired into his laptop. He could control how fast the panels lit up and in what order the sequence appeared. He showed me my job. If blue lit up, I tapped blue ASAP. That extinguified the blue light and another colour panel lit up like a traffic light on speed.

Purple, then yellow, lit up till I tapped them out. The four colours began to appear, in random order, faster and faster till my paws were a blur as I tapped the lit-up panels. Then Goldenboy attached little wooden drumsticks to my paws with silver Velcro. The drumsticks worked great for tapping. The computer showed my reaction time. Cats are usually right around 0 to 70 milliseconds (0 to .07 seconds). Blinking your eye takes. 1 millisecond. I was quick ... as a cat (duh). With my drumsticks I was lightning fast (.06 seconds), and I soon figured out the sequence and pattern of the lights.

With my drumsticks I was a regular Ringo Starr. Goldenboys plan was to train me ½ hour daily and the have me compete with an untrained cat at the Sinus Fair (Slick?)

The other half of the study would involve the righting reflex of a cat (me) dropped from a height. (up to

117

30 feet) To do this, Goldenboy planned to build a volcano which would erupt (a Sinus Fair golden oldie) while simultaneously cat-a-pultifying me thirty feet in the air. My job (if I dared) would be to deftly right myself in the air and land gently on a foam pad after the descent. Goldenboy would use a host of movie cameras hooked to his computer to document my flite including: height in the air, initial muzzle velocity, my body position, my maximumified falling speed and the degree of terror on my face (and my degree of continence).

Goldenboy used a lot of euphemistifying language explaining this to me, carefully avoiding words like exploding, cat-a-pulting and falling. I figured it out myself by analizifying the neat sketches and drawings on his desktop. I wondered about Term Life Insurance. But you know, I had savified my go-nads... why not live a little.

Just when my life as a sinus experiment testee was wrapping up, Goldenboy added, "And Gloomer wants to compare the effects of Meowijuana (designer catnip from Amazon) versus real marijuana on a boy cat. Goldenboy had noticed thet my ever-present go-nads had NOT left the building. The only thing neutered for me was my enthusiasm for flight. (I figured Gloomer was in it for the weed – she was not curiosified like me and Goldenboy).

Being an adventurer at heart, I nodded at Goldenboy and mewed and purred something sounding like, "Hey, this sounds like fun." Goldenboy was building a six-foot high paper-mashee Volcano that would eruptify violently from a mixture of baking soda (sodium bicarbonate) and vinegar (aqueous acetic acid … Google) mixed with red dye to give the eruptifying foamy stuff the look and color of real salava (molten rock… Google). He called his volcano Mount Stromboli after the volcanic island near Sicily (a mob volcano) which eruptified in 2002, 2003, 2007, 2013 and 2014. (a frequent flyer.)

What would give our project the winning edge would be me … cat- a-pulted outa a round 10 inch diameter vent hidden in the side of the volcano away from the judges. The cat-a-pult would be powered by 10 stretched ½ inch lab hoses stretched by a crank wheel and released by a small red 'Ejectify Button." All the motion activated cameras on poles (the posts, not the nationality) would catch my fight up through the erupting 'salava" to captify my courage for posterity and beyond.

Gloomer's interest was to have me fly before and after Meowi-wanna, to measure the effect of catnip on cat flight. To be continued … Impaired flight sounded riskified to me. "And that's why you should never fly when stoned." (Sully S.)

Chapter 15

A trip to the Gym with Afrodite and Sven's Sexy Seven

"I was kicked out of college for cheating on the meta-physics exam: I looked into the soul of another student."—Woody Allen

I figured I would take a night off the prowl to rest up after my near castration mini-nightmare. I was bored as hell, but used the time to check out Rosa's part of the manshun. Rosa took a night off every month to visit family and friends at the Guacamolan Social Club in downtown Pittsburg. They ate a lot of Guacamolan food: Tostadas (toast), tamales (meat wrapped in corn dough pancakes and banana leaves), Pepian (spicified chikun stew with red peppers and tomatos), Hilachas (shredded beef stew with potatos and carrots in sauce ... spicified) and of course beans, corn, and more corn pancakes. Dessert was Mole de Plantanos. (fried bananas dipped in Chocolate... Google)

Of course, they had dancing and singing (some old Mayan folk songs like Guantanemola) and lots of Guacamolan Gallo brewskis. Little Rosa could slam them back almost as fast as Fishface ... but would never throw a cat. I suspect that Rosa no longer detested me. 'The enemy of my enemy is my friend.' (The General)

Rosa drove a 1990 Ford Pinto, which Velcrodome let her park behind the 4 garages. (covered with a tarp... to save the paint job). She drove into town to celebrate with her Guacamolan pals and returned in the morning, when she sobered up, to cook our breakfast.

Velcrodrome had converted the fifth garage space into a weeny 10 by 12 foot apartment for Rosa. She was happy with a concrete floor. She wove beautiful wall hangings and carpets out of bright dyed strips of banana leaves to make the colorful designs. Her apartment, with a bed and a chair and a toilet and sink was comfifyed. I searched her dresser drawers to see if I could find either a current Guacamolan Passport or Visa papers. Nothin! She was probably an illegal immigrant, but I liked her command of Spanish cuss words. She could stay!

With a good night's rest, I was up early. I wanted to see what Afrodite, my darling, did all day! Her real name was Gwendolin Shultz. She had not changed her name when Velcrodome (Friedrich Shultz) changed his handle to Woodrow Studley Woodbridge. After a hearty breakfast of a Kale smoothie and 4 almonds, Afrodite, who was sporting a bright yellow spandex full-body suit grabbed her gym bag and headed for the garage. She was taking a selfie to check her makeup as she headed for the gleaming silver Mercedees mothership. I easily slipped through the open door and staked myself out in the SUB's vast rear storage area, ready to observe.

"I am on the edge of mysteries and the veil is getting thinner and thinner." Louie Pasturize

Her workouts happened at "Sven's Super Spa and Gym... Yoga and More." The spa was located at a shopping center fifteen minutes from Fox Chapel Hill Gated Community.

She checked her makeup again with a selfie as we entered the gym which was quite spacious. The exercise facility had a big central yogi studio with mega poster pictures of some body-builder blonde dude in spandex with a man-bun in various yogi poses. In the giant photos the 'Man-hunk' demonstrated Yogi poses: Downward-facing Dog, the Humpy Camel, the Tired Turtle, The Bard of Paradise, the Crow, the Eagle, the Pregnant Stork, the Wounded Budgie and course , The Mariachi-Yasana pose (The pose I assume to lick my strokum when it's itchy. The Nature Channel).

Along the back wall were two large change rooms... One labelled 'Women' and one labelled, 'The Sven Sexy Seven Only.' There was no change room for men.

Afrodite smiled warmly and gave an enthusiastified wave to the blond guy with a man-bun dressed in a bright powder blue spandex body-suit, sitting in the office.

"Hey, Sven. Hope you are horny! It's Tuesday!", she bubbled. Sven's sculpted face erupted into a big toothy smile (I wished I had sunglasses) and nodded, "Alvaysss!" He had to be Scandalavian. (Sven in Svedish means 'Young warrior. Google)

In the center of the back wall of the yogi studio was a huge banner in Svedish colors (yellow and blue) saying "Sven's Sexy Seven." Beneath the banner were full body photos shots of seven gorgeous women all wearing brightly-coloured full-body yogi spandex posing as lewdly as possible. Front and center was old Afrodite, looking flawless and sexy. The other six looked like the rest of the Miami Dolphins cheerleading squad: tall, lithe, athletified, and stacked like corned beef sandwiches.

There was one orientified woman and one Latinified women in the midst of the five beautiful blondies. Possibly, the Sven Seven were chosen for something other than their Mensa status; Mensa- types are usually snobs.

Soon, about fifteen, middle-aged, ordinary, suburpanite females emerged from the 'Womans" change-room, mostly wearing Lulu Lemonade sweat pants and bright T-shirts with their little tummies hangin out. A few of them started doing little jumps and deep breathing.

A sportified younger woman, who was stretching out her legs, whined, "Goddam, I am so stiff! Sven was a bruuut, yesterday!"

Next, old Sven, his muscles shining in the bright sunshine, burst outa his office doing jumping jacks and flexing his biceps. It looked like he had stuffed two pair of sweat socks plus a giant carrot under his bodysuit in the crotch area... as if to say, "Plezzed to meet cha, middle-aged vimin! "

The regular suburpinite women were, by now, jumping up and down and clapping and giggling while staring at Sven's crotch. He jocked-walked over to "The Sven Seven's Dressing Room" and tapped firmly on the door ....

"My zesty Vimin, Ve avait the pleashur of your company. Now, Hit ze mat, Sven's Seven. Yaw! Ve Vill not Vait!"

Sven's Seven bopped outa the dressing room wearing matching skintight body suits in the colors of the rainbow. A strong olfartry wave of pricey perfume; Tom Ford meets Coco Channel overwhelmed the already existing strong odor of Brut (Sven, I guess) and old sweat. Talk about color co-ordinated: violet, indigo, blue, green, yellow, orange and red.

Their tight butts and surgically enhancified boobs jiggled in unisom, like the fiddling section of the Philli Harmonified Orchestra.

The normal, middle-aged suburpinites all sucked in their guts in a desperate attempt to slimify.

Sven bust into serious stretching exercises at the front of the group. "Stretch, stretch, stretch all zoess muscles girls... Yaw! Zee hamstrings. Yaw! Zee quadiceps! Zee biceps and, Yaw! Zee triceps. Zee rhomboids and Yaw, Zee latissimus Dorsey." Old Sven knew his female anatomy. The normal women were wheezing. The Sven Seven were loving it. Svens carrot, which had originally been pointing true north was now pointing north-west. I resisted the urge to bite it...

My vegan thoughts were interrupted when Sven suddenly spun his lithe body into the Mariachi-Yasimified pose. (My strokum-licking favorite). This complex pose involved: start on your back then lift your butt off the floor until your butt points to the ceiling. Then, trying not to fart, flip your legs over till your knees are on both sides of your head. You can picture the value of this pose in licking your balls with your raspy tongue.

I was observing, innocently, from the top of the Sven's Special Vitamin cabinet, nibbling on Sven's tuna salad lunch. Sven used the Mariachi pose to adjust his carrot back to true north. The regular suburpinites were sweating and gasping for oxygen. One of them farted rapidly nine times like a bass drummer with epilepsy. A smell, like dead river carp meets mustard gas, crept thru the room. Even Sven's Seven were soon gasping and choking in a search for fresh air.

Sven said, "Somebodee cut ze cheese in here, Yaw!" The offending party soon cleared out to the dressing room, looking embarified. Sven poured on the heat: stretching, bending, flexing, strengthening, jumping, leaping, twisting and running on the spot. Even the Sven Seven were busting into a sweat. The suburpinites were a hot, sweaty mess.

Sven's carrot looked like it had become deturgified by sweat and was drooping in a southern direction. I finished off Sven's tuna lunch... those Scandalavians ate a lotta fish.

Sven clapped for the ladies and bowed, "Good verk, vimin. You verked hard. See you in ze morning, same time in ze same place. Eat vell and schleep vell. Gute nacht und Bis morgan! (Good night and see you tomorrow! German... Rosetta's Stones.)

I assumed the carrot would be Sven's lunch. I waited around for Afrodite for at least half an hour. The suburpinites straggled out in clusters, still sweating, chatting about kids and soccer and teachers at the local high school. Sven's Seven emerged next, freshly showered in fresh designer clothes with perfect hair and makeup, chatting in groups of two and three. Their favorite topic was the cost of local Botox, followed by butt lift or not, liposuction, nannies, domestic help, and Sven's carrot.

Afrodite was the last of the Sven Seven outa of the dressing Room. I figured she might have been holding back a big dump. She was all gussied up, of course, but she was dressed in a very skimpified maid's outfit (and not one of Rosa's). I figured maybe she had taken a little part-time work to suppliment V-Domes magnificent cash flow.

My dilemma was resolvified when old Sven emerged from his office, freshly showered, with his shining hair falling like a golden waterfall over his muscular neck and shoulders. (EYHORF- eat our heart out Robert Frost)

Sven was as naked as a Jaybird! As he stepped from his office, the sun came out and a beam of sunlight illuminated his robust physique. He was a Viking God. And that thingy in his crotch was NOT a carrot and two pair of sweatsocks. Sven was hung... like fucking Northern Dancer. (proud winner of the Triple Crown of Horseracing in 1973 and star of the Disney Movie 'Northern Dancer' Wicked-pedia)

Afrodite lept into Sven's arms and the couple retreated to the Svedish Massage area behind Sven's office. Afrodite spotted me and said, "Get the fuck outa here, you fucking cat."

Why did that name stick to me like Elmo's glue?

Editors note: I am back... you signed a contract, asshole. You are called TFC because that is incisively correct.

Arthurs Note: Shutup, You no-it-all, STFU!

The sound effects emanating from that room would make a porno star blush. I won't go there for the sake of any children under 30 reading this book. (Parents... DYKWYKisR... Do You Know What Your Kid is Reading)

Arthurs note: Part of my huge profits from this best-seller will go to my favorite charities, Cats against Porn (CAP) and Cats against Male Wigs that look like Dead Mammals (CAMWTLLDM).

That Sven had stamina. I was more of a sprinter myself. They emerged from the Svedish Massage Room, sweating and smiling 45 minutes later.

Sven said, "That vas vonderfull, Darlink! Vill I see you for another session on Tursday?"

Afrodite slapped his toned butt and giggled like a teenager, "You betcha, Buster."

Now I knew why Afrodite liked yogi so much.

Chapter 16

The Sinus Experiment Shapifies

"Science is the great antidote to the poison of enthusiasm and superstition."—Adam Smith

Rosa fed me sardines (Yum) and a big bowl of cream when we returned to the manshun.

She greated me, "Oye, El gato maravilloso? como estan colando? ("Hey, wondercat. How are they hanging?" Rosetta's stones.) She nodded at Afrodite who was eating a pickle for lunch, "Oye, zorra, ? te follaste hoy? Eso espero." ("Hey, slut. Did you get banged today? Hope so." Rosetta's stones.)   That Guacamolan illegal immigrunt had a nastified tongue on her.

I retired to my sunroom where I had a serious nap for two hours till I heard the teenagers returning home from school. They were both speaking Spanish. Goldenboy had immersed himself in Spanish via Khan Acadamy over the last week. I suspected he had a very high IQ (probably over 180... like me) and a sharpified memory. He ate a triple-dekker PB and J sandwich (Sourdough) and slurpified a big glass of chocolate milk to fortify himself for our lab session.

The volcano looked just like Mount Stromboli in the ocean off Sicily (a Mob vacation spot). It stood six feet tall and was all painted grey, like rocks, with red and black salava flowing down the steep slopes. The biggest volcanic explosion in history was Crak-a toe-a, Indianasia, which erupted in 1883 with 13,000 times the force of the USA bomb that blew up in Hero-shima to end WW2 in 1945. (Wicked-pedia). Goldenboy opened a trap door into the base of the Volcano and showed me the big metal baking pan for mixing the chemicals and red dye to create the salava. The molton salava emptied, under expansion pressure, through a plastic shoot made from 2 litre Coke bottles (V-Dome loved Coca-Cola) to deliver the Salava to the hole in the top of the volcano, called a caldera. (Nature Channel)

He showed me the cat-a-pult and flyer-cat-cavity (CFCC) built into the slope of the volcano. My flyer cavity was ten-inch diameter vertical hole in the mountain out of which I would be violently ejected, like bacon at a Bar-Mitzva.

Then he showed me my flying outfit- which was seriously cool: a shiny silver crash helmet with a pull down visor like Formula 1 Race drivers wear, a silver cape (which looked mighty fine against my dark rosetified fur), and silver boots. (EYHOMA... Eat Your Heart Out Mario Andretti).

Editor's Note: I quit again.

Arthur's Note: You are fired again. I fire you! He-he-he.

Finally, Gloomer came in and introduced me to my new Catnip toy ... It was a pink chewable pseudo-rat full of catnip, with a bottle of Kong's Natural Catnip spray to increase the dose of catnip , as she wished.

I love catnip. Nepata cataria is a plant known as catnip, cats wort, or Catmint. (Wicki) The active drug in catnip is nepetalactone which is absorbed by smell (olfartry absorption). Cats, even lions and jaguars, love catnip. It stimulates the 'Happy Receptors" in the cat brain and works for 5-15 minutes after sniffing or eating it. Cats mellow right out right after catnip exposure. An overdose can cause severe puking and diarrhea. I was not sure about mixing catnip and flight.

Goldenboy cheerfully announced. "Ok, Trial run on Saturday." Goldenboy and I practiced on the drum-stick and rotating lights thingy for 10 minutes. My reaction time was down to .05 seconds

Chapter 17

Another Night on the Town: Why are Housecats Moronified Losers

"You are the product of 4 billion years of evolutionary success. Fucking act like it."—Anon

I slept through supper and by the time I woke up it was dark outside. I had missed my friend Slick and had been eating like a housecat for a day. Gloomer had given me a coupla hits of catnip – which gave me a wee buzz, but put me right to sleep. It was a drowsifying trip for me. Fishface's Marijuwana had similar effects on this Tomcat. I vowed to avoid cat flight while stoned.

I left the manshun and headed craftily across the yards and meadows for the big maple where I hoped to find Slick. I kept a close eye above and behind me for that nasty Giant Hornified Owl who had taken one of my lives. Slick had not arrived yet. I snacked on a few sparrows and a tasty robin while I waited, thinking about the age old question,

"Why are most house cats moronified losers?"

To answer the question I had to examine the history of Domesticated cats. The original cats (felis catus) were African wild cats who were wild carnivorous predatory hunters. The Egyptians 'adopted' the 'nicer' wildcats into their farming communities to be 'mousers' and 'ratters'.

They hung out near the grain storage areas and were venerated (loved and respected) by the Egyptians who spent most of their time supervising their slaves, who constructified the Pyramids. When the Egyptians and the Catholicks got turned off cats (witches and cats), they killed both and Bazinga! - the rat and mouse population in Europe and Asia and North Africa went bananas. Then, next thing you know, the Black (Boobonic Plague) Death, caused by a bacteria (yersinia peste) spread rampantly by bites from infected mice or rats. The Black Death killed almost 200 million human beans from 1347 to 1351. (Google)

Predatory (natural) cats, like me, might have prevented the Plague by killing off the rodents. (Fun fact... Cats can get the Plague too... Wiki).

The total calamity of cats happened when they moved inside, to live with the human beans. Humans then started trying to selectively breed cats with pointy ears, or softer coats, or green eyes, or passive temperments. Soon you had as many as 73 specific breeds of pedigreed domestic cats. (The International Cat Association)

The result is $500 Siamese kitten who wants to spend her life inside an apartment on an old lady's lap.

In the mid 1900's they started chopping off cats' go-nads shortly after birth to 1) further pacify the house pet and 2) stop unwanted litters of cats popping out. (Wicky)

So, human beans domesticated us, but they totally changed our behavior and our lives. They fed us a can of Whiskas Chikun Science diet food with hairball control every day and kept us inside a tiny apartment 24/7. It's like raising a shark in a bathtub. They took away everything that was fun: hunting, exploring, fucking and fighting and turned us into mewing, purring Fluffballs with hairballs to meet their needs.

Honestly, all cats are narcissistic sociopaths deep down, as are all true predators. We can take human beans or ignore them... 'Meh!'

Losing our collective go-nads was the beginning of the end of the good life for felis catus. I plan to hang on to mine... and wear them out if possible.

"Live Free or Die." (Written on Braveheart's license plate after he moved to New Hampshire).

While on the topic of cats and go-nads, here is something deeply ironified; human beans are pissed at cats because they kill at least 2 billion (up to 4 billion) wild birds a year in the USA. Small wild birds are mostly feathers... forget the owls and eagles w ho are too nasty to kill. The average American human bean eats 7000 whole animals: 11 cows, 27 pigs, 2400 chickens, 80 turkeys, 30 sheep 4500 fish over a human lifetime. Human beans around the world also eat 30 million dogs and 10 million cats per year. We snack on birds and they pig out on animals. (Swine is the #1 meat)

At least cats get some exercise. Humans should become vegetarians to solve the problem of killing fellow animals. Cats are obligated carnivores. Modern human beans are all either lactose- intolerant, glucose-intolerant, gluten-sensified or allergic to nuts and shellfish. Whole foods is working on dairy-free cows and McDonalds has a new burger called 'The Big Whoop' with nothin but a bun, lettuce and fake catsup. Cats are not the problem.

A deep voice arrested my reverie, "Hey, kid, How's life?" I stammered, "Ah, great, Slim. And you?" Slim had startled me. He said, "Ya know, livin the dream."

Fortunately we both spoke the same dialect of Catonese, the universal cat language that included a lot of body language, growls, purrs, meows and subtle grunts, moans and occasionally howls. Compared to me, Slick was a Tomcat of mighty few words. I explained my close brush with being castratified to Slick who mumbled, "Fucking vets, why don't they stick to cows." He said, "Felix, we are backordered on horny Queens at the trailer park. Hope your boys are fully recovered." I said, "Bring em on, Slick." And did a little happy dance in the moon-light.

We proceeded to another good hunting spot beside a leaky granary about ten minutes away. The place was buzzing with field mice and some large rattus rattus specimins. We chased, tormented, killed and ate the little buggers till we were satisfied.

Slick took me into the hay shed and showed me how to stalk and kills barn swallows by climbing across the high beams to attack them where they rested and slept. A barn swallow has a nice, salty, crunchy flavor once you get past the feathers.

We headed for the Slumber Safe trailer Park for some con-sexual coitus with a host of horney Queens.

You would think we were selling the new iPhone 23... we were that popular. I felt like a rock star. Again, for the sake of children under 30, I will skip the most lurid details of our vigorous copulatory success. The only swimmers I had left by the end of the night were doing the dead man's float. My go-nads were feeling like they had run a marathon. I had pledged to wear them out... but not in a week.

I wandered back to the manshun for some cream and a well- earned sleep.

Chapter 18

Felix Goes Hi-Tech and Considers Spiritual Matters

"Stripping away the irrational, the illogical and the impossible, I am left with atheism. I can live with that."
—Mark Twain

When I awoke, Rosa and Afrodite were finishing breakfast. Afrodite was actually eating a piece of toast with butter with her kale smoothy. Feeling reckless, I guessed. Rosa was polishing off a big plate of huevos ranchera. She ate with Mucho gusto. (Spanish "mucho gusto" ... Felix)

Afrodite said, "So the soiree (fancy party) will be simple. Only about fifty people. We will get a caterer for the food... heavy hor'durvs and low-cal desserts (a foxy-moron). Fred (she called V- Dome Fred... behind his back) will make the 12 most beautiful of the 57 Starstuds managers attend to be our wait staff. We will have a full bar with a little fashion show for the "Sven Sexy Seven." I have sent the invites for a week Saturday night at 7 pm which gives time to shop for a new designer outfit. The dress code will be 'Casually Elegant.'"

Rosa scowled, "Cierta, senora. ?Y quien diablos se encarga de limpiar el disaster." ("Right, lady. And who the hell gets to clean up the mess?" ... Rosetta's Stones.)

Afrodite took off for a haircut and a mani-pedi appointment and her Yogi work-out. It was Thursday, and she had her massage session with Sven. I had done the math on the Sven Seven. Someone was getting stiffed because Afrodite got second helpings each week. However, as one of the two tomcat studs of Slumber Safe Trailer Park, I was in no moral or ethical position to castify stones! (the Bible)

I had a sound sleep till 2 PM, then Googled my brains out for a few hours. I had wangled an iPad outa Goldenboy, who obviously wanted to keep me happy till he shot me out of his volcano a few times. The iPad touch screen worked great with my velroed drumsticks. My learning curve was exponentified even further.

143

I discovered I could order stuff on amazon on V-Dome's credit card. I was soon a Prime Member and had downloaded a Kindle reader for my fiction and non-fiction needs. V-Dome's password was easy… Stud57 and his email was Studley57@gmail.com. What a moron. I had started to write this very book on Word on Goldenboy's iPad. (EYHOEH … Eat Your Heart Out Earnest Hemingway) Earnest was a cat-lover!

I ordered a new 2022 Apple iPad Pro (12.9 inch, wi-fi + cellular, 128 GB, M1 chip, Liquid Retina display) in purple, my favorite colour. It had touch ID. I added two ipad pencils (to upgrade my Velcroed drumsticks) and a Smart keyboard. "Go big or go home." Felix the Tomcat (TFC) The package came in at less than two grand. V-Dome, who was skimming at least 10 grand cash a day from his 57 'Starstuds and More' outlets would not notice a couple grand on his Visa card.

We Prime members got same-day delivery. I would pick that puppy off the porch when I spotted the Amazon van which spent most of the day in the Fox Chapel Hill Gated Community, delivering more shit to people who already had way too much shit. I knew that none of my self-absorbed Guppie family would notice a new computer – except Goldenboy, who could borrow it from time-to-time (he alreadyhad seven iPads).

Goldenboy and me were texting back and forth a few times daily so I sent him a picture of my new iPad. He sent me back a text with a happy-face emoji with-in seconds with,

'My man Felix. Yeah!' Goldenboy had my back.

"The cat is the best anarchist."

"A cat has absolute honesty." (Both by Earnest Hemingway)

My inner voice asked myself the honest question, "Felix the Tomcat. Honestly, are you an anarchist or are you becoming a Guppy?" My other inner anarchist/jaguar voice replied,

"Fuck you, Felix's other inner voice! Don't, make me cross over (via the corpus callosum) to your side of the brain to explain this to you." I was safe! Fuck the Guppies, too!

I had a nice nap, knowing that my sharpified hearing would detect the sound of the Amazon van delivering my new iPad. I got a few $20 bills out of V-Domes top dresser drawer to tip the Amazon driver. They did not mind a little spit on their cash. There had to be 10 k in $50s and $20s in V-Dome's drawer. He ought to investify in a decent wig that did not look like a dead rodent. God only knew what was in the little steel safe in his massive walk-in closet.

Anyway, when I woke up before Goldenboy got home. He was in the 'Nerds of the North' club at school. The young brainiacs were trying to build a quantum Computer, which was beyond my high-tech know-how.

Q: "Why did Schroedinger have an open casket funeral?

A: To be there…or not." (anon)

I fired up my current iPad Pro (3rd generation) and Googled 'Religions of the World." I was curious. Up popped a U-Tube program called "The Story of God" with Morgan Freedom. I loved his deep voice, which reminded me of Slick and Hank. I loved old Morgan in "Shawshanks Redemptified" where he and a skinny criminal, Tim Robber, I think, bust outa prison to re-capture a whole load of cash that they had previously stolen and hidden in Mexico. I won't tell you the ending, in case you haven't seen it on Netflicks.

Anyway, I got a good summary of religion, over history, from old Morgan in the next hour. It was fascinating.

Basically, it appears, mankind (or womankind) dreamed up God to make themselves feel better when they realized that they were all doomed to certain croakification. (Death) "Death and Taxes, yada, yada." Felix the Tomcat

So, the Jews created and worshipified Yahwaa (since 10,000 years ago) and the Hindus worshipified many Deeities (since 6000 years ago) including Krishna, Shiva, Rama and old Durga. Hindus believe in Karma (ya get what ya deserve). The Buddists (since 1700 years ago did not really believe in a God, but were wild about this guy Budda, the canary-eater who you met in Chapter Three). I liked Budda plenty.

The biggest and most powerful group (especially in Red states) were the Christians (2.2 billion in the world) who dominated world religion for the last 2200 years. They worshipped the Trinity... Three Gods who were all in the same family ... (nepotismic) - a Dad God, a Son God and a Mother God (with no stretch marks).

Anyway there are 34,000 different brands of Christianity, most of whom believed that they were right about everything and that everyone else in the world was wrong. The different factions enjoyed scrapping with each other over who their preachers could have sex with. Sometimes those tiffs explodified into real wars. Some Christians disapproved of all kinds of stuff: divorce, alcohol, gay people, smoking, dancing and having fun. In every religion there were lots of folks who pretended to believe so they could play on the church's baseball team and attend potluck suppers.

Finally, there were the Moslems since 700 AD (1.9 billion) who are something like Christians with a different Holy Book, a different leader and plenty of automatic wepuns. Christians also enjoy automatic wepuns, but mostly in the Red states, where everyone has them. There were two big branches of Moslems, called Shias and Sunnys, who tended to hate eachothers' guts. Anyway, I gotta stop this write-up because they might put out a Fatwah on me. (Like a hit, man!)

Remember Felix, you are at 5 ½ lives. So, shutup already. Muslims are against humor (Salmon Rushday) and seeing women's faces (enuf said).

My favorite religion is the JW-yahs (8.5 million). They believe in door-to-door sales of free pamplets and in getting doors slammed in their faces every Saturday morning. They do the door-to- door stuff, faithfully, to get magic brownie points (with God) counting toward winning one of the 144,000 spots in JW-Yah heaven (Do the math folks!).

Q: "What do you get when you cross a JW-Yah with a Hell's Angel?"

A: "A kid who knocks on your door and tells you to 'Fuck Off'."

Our Hell's Angels' Security team here, in Fox Chapel Gated Community have a belief; their Faith leads them to kick JW-yahs and Moremans in the ass if they show up at the Pearly Green Gates.

Moremans, like the fish monger in Chapter Two, were similar to the JW-yahs but had a bunch of wives and about a zillion kids. Instead of going door-to-door to spread their faith, they head back to the bedroom for another roll-in-the-hay. (talk about organic growth of a religion).

And, of course, you have your Atheists (ain't no god), your Agnostics (God... maybe, maybe not), your polytheists (lotsa gods), your pantheists (gods in all natural things) and your anti-god types who preferred Satan (God's nemesis). And finally, you had your modern narssisified materialists (Is there a What?... sorry, gotta take this call) who worship stuff and money as their God (like V-Dome, Afrodite and many of their fellow Guppies).

Morgan Freedom was an agnostic (God... maybe, maybe not)- so I joined that church too. I liked that they didn't make you feel guilty for skippin church on Friday or Saturday or Sunday and DID NOT ASK FOR MONEY.

"Religion was invented when the first con man met the first fool." (Mark Twain)

"God loves you, and He needs MONEY." (George Carlin)

Editors Note: I predicted Felix would ultimately offend everyone... remember, all of your complaints and hate mail go to: FelixtheTomcat2022@outlook.com. LMTFO (Leave me the fuck out)

Arthurs Note: I told you I would offend everyone. You are welcome.

Anyway, after refraction, I identified the worst of the religious folks... the Catholicks. The average Catholick was probably just fine... but their leadership, the Cardinals and the Pope, all living it up in luxury in Rome, had caused much of the trouble in history. Everything from the Crusades 1091 to 1295 (murder Moslems), to the Spanish Inquisition 1470s (murder Jews, Muslims and witches). Witches were mostly women with warts who could not swim.

Anyway the Catholicks backed off in the last few hundred years and switched to molestifying alterboys and taming indigenous tribes by reprograming their kids as Catholicks in creepy residential boarding schools. The Catholic leadership sucks big-time!

My conclusion: Religion creates little clubs (who mostly hate eachother) who offer the illusion of piece-of-mind and eternal life in Heaven in return for taking your money to build fancy churches and hire preachers (who work one day a week... a good gig).

Since 85% percent of the world's human beans say they have a religion, I suspect that I, Felix the Tomcat, have finally screwed the pooch. (metaphorically, not literally.)

Editor's Note: Way to go Felix, you Asshole. WTF. I quit.

Arthurs Note: Whoops! Dear Readers... the next few chapters are really fun... about (maybe) me going over Niagara Falls and about the Sinus Experiment in which I am totally wrecked by being shot out of Goldenboy's Volcano and (maybe) die. I am shown to be a stupid Asshole. (Karma)

Editor's Note: You are an asshole, Felix. Karma should beat your ass.

Arthurs Note: I have just embracified Buddhism (Namastay). I might start my own religion where you just sit around and laugh at jokes and drink alcoholified beverages.

Editors Note: Sorry Felix, that religion is taken... it is called 'Pubism.' (PuhBism , not PooBism)

Arthurs Note: WTF. Readers, turn the page. I dare you! There is a free coupon for a new cryptocurrency (called Felixbucks) at the end of the book. Redeemable at any Weedshop.

"Lord, help us to be the people our dogs think we are." (Anon)

Chapter 19

On The Road Again

"On the road again

Like a band of gypsies we go down the highway

We're the best of friends

Insisting that the world keep turning our way

And our way

Is on the road again."—Willie Nelson

Slick, Hank and me were on the road again and Willie was just whaling away on the cassette player in the old Peterbuilt Truck. Hank was piloting us to Niagara Falls, Canada. We had a huge load of hay on the back... hard to grow hay Canada because of snow. Hank was singing along. Hank had a pretty good bass voice that complimentified Willie's reedy tenor. Slick and I were cat line-dancing on the passenger seat. Cats do not have to wear seat belts. We were snacking on a 454 gram tub of Temptation Cat treats and Hank was knawing on salted peanuts. The guy could still sing great with a mouth full of peanuts. I knew 'the Hindlick' from 'ER reruns'.

The trip to the Falls was only 250 miles from Pittsburg... about 5 hours up the interstate thru Erie, Pennsylvania. I was looking forward to seeing Lake Erie, the eleventh largest lake in the world (Great Lakes... Wiki).

When Hank was not singing along to Willie, Merle (Hazard), or Jonny (Cash), he was talkin... non-stop. Hank provided a running salilokey.

A salilokey is like Shakaspear's Hamlet ... "Out damn Spot." Hamlet had a dog. Hank liked to ask himself interesting questions and then he tried to answer them.

Hank asked, "Is Hilary really a witch?"

Hank replied, "The wart on her nose says 'yes' but Bill says 'No', not a witch... a bitch."

Hank asked, "Why am I driving to Canada to see Freeda, my religious JW-Yah sister who is certifiably nuts?"

Hank growled, "I have to help her throw my dad's ashes over the Falls... Duh! And it's the Lord's will."

Hank asked, "Why did Daddy leave Freeda the house and me a fucking 80-year-old shotgun?"

Hank answered, "Because she was always the 'good kid' and I was the 'rebel.' Also, Canadians don't need to shoot eachother like we do in the US of A."

I was enjoying the banter between Hank and Hank. I had downloadified a new machine-learning App for my iPad called 'Speechify Text to Speech' which could translate up to 800 written words per minute into any of 14 spoken languages (including Chinese, Spanish and Svedish with 130+ voices including officially licensed Gyneth Pulcratrow. (of Vagina Rocks Fame) and Morgan Freedom.

"Speechify lets me listen to hundreds of GROOP blog posts out loud in the car." (Gwyneth Pulcratrow)

If I had Speecify working and had 300 words per minute typing speed I could run for President. (Independent) I would not join any political party that would allow me to join. With Speechify I could literally be a university perfesser... Doctor Felix. (Cat History)

As Hank droned on, Slick fell asleep and I was lost in the music. I enjoyed Gordon Lightfeet singin,

"In the early morning rain with a dollar in my hand

With an aching in my heart and my pockets full of sand

I'm a long way from home, Lord, I miss my loved ones so

In the early morning rain with no place to go..." (Gordon Lightfoot)

And I thought my Karma sucked. Poor guy... chest pain, stuck in the rain, homeless with only a buck. Good thing he was a Canuck... free health care, easy welfare and lots of Dollar stores.

Soon we hit the Canadian border at Niagara Falls, New York and got on the bridge over the river to Niagara Falls, Canada. (confusing).

I expected to see my first Mountie (RCMP... Royal Canadian Mounted Police) and my first horse.

I was disappointed; the Canadian border guards looked like the US border guards, with better hygiene (mostly women). They were polite and finished every sentence with "Aye". "Good day, sir. Nice weather, aye. Whatcha got as your cargo? Hay, aye. Any cats in the truck? No? OK, aye. You can drive thru." Hank, who was pretty deaf, replied, "Aye?"

We crossed into Canada. Niagara Falls, Canada looked just like the US side, with no snow and no flags.

It was equally tacky. Most of the people looked Asian and they all had iPhone cameras on little sticks, snappifying grinnified photos of themselves blocking out the Falls.

We got a glimpse of the Canadian Falls (Horseshoe Falls) which were at least 50 times bigger and better than the wimpy US falls. We sped through town and Hank dropped the hay off at a big farm about five miles outa town. We were going to see his nutty sister Freeda and her crazy husband, Mike. Mike was that Uncle... the one nobody ever invited to weddings.

Mike was a 'Furry'... 'an enthusiast for animal characters with human characteristics, in particular, a person who dresses up in animal costumes and has an animal persona called a fursona." (WebMD)

When we arrived at their crappy-looking bungalow about a mile from the falls, there was a six-foot Beagle dog cutting firewood in the driveway. Hank parked the truck in the nearby schoolyard (it was Saturday) and we walked back to the house. The Beagle looked-up and wagged its tail. It gave a few happy barks and licked Hank on the face. It said, "Hey Hank, welcome to Canada, aye." I figured that Beagle son-of-a-bitch already had 'Speechify'.

Suddenly, the Beagle took its head off (not easy without oppossified thumbs) and waved toward the house, "The bitch is inside, aye."

A chubby woman with frizzified hair raced to the door and hugged Hank,

"Hey, big brother. Welcome to Canada, aye! Did ya see the falls on the way over. Aye?"

Hank said, "Yup. Still in the same place."

Freeda was all bubbly and excited to see her older brother.

"Hey, Hank. How is Franny? Aye!" Franny was Hanks ex-wife. They were no kids.

'Ain't seen her in 10 years, Freeda. Hope it stays that way."

"Who are these delightful companions, Hank. Aye?"

Hank said, "Coupla cats."

The Beagle, who had listened silently till this point said, "Woof. Woof."

Freda gave him a 'Milkbone doggy treat' which he swallowed whole. Then the beagle got down on the floor and rolled over, which ain't easy for a six-foot Beagle in a small kitchen. Freeda served Hank and herself a big lunch... tomato soup and balonie sandwiches. She put bread and balonie and mustard in a big metal bowl on the floor for her husband, who went by the dog name 'Yoda'. Yoda scarfified his lunch greedily in about 4 ½ seconds. Yoda spent the rest of lunch eye-balling Hank's baloni, wagging his tail. Slick and me each gobblified a small bowl of baloni and some cream I had to bite the Beagle in the ass twice to keep him outa my lunch. I loved baloni. Afrodite never bought that stuff… probably a Canadian delicassy like Back Bacon, aye!

After lunch, Freeda stood up and said, "Hey, family… let's go dump Daddy's ashes over the falls, aye. The Lord told me that today is the day, aye." She pointed at a giant urn with a Canadian flag on it sitting on the kitchen counter beside the toaster.

Hank said, "OK." And Yoda wagged his tail and said, "Woof, woof."

Yoda had put the Beagle head back on. He was in full 'Fursona'.

We trooped off to the falls. We took a city bus. The driver looked suspiciously at Yoda.

"Are you a senior, sir? Aye?"

Freeda said, "No, but he thinks he's a fucking Beagle!"

The Falls were busy … lots of visitors, all busy shoving and pushing to get a spot at the metal railing keeping tourists from falling into the river and going over the falls. (behind Casinos, suicide is the second biggest industry in Niagara Falls, Canada).

Mist rose from the massive Niagara George. The waterfall thundered almost 500 feet to crash into the turbulence below. There was some guy driving a boat around below the falls... musta taken a right instead of a left in Toronto. Anyway, the falls were fantastic.

Freeda was elbowing Asians outa the way to get to the metal rail so she could chuck her dear Daddy's ashes into the river to send him over the falls. (A common Canadian dying wish..."Hey, send me over the falls when I die, aye!") She said a brief prayer. Slick and I crossed ourselves and Yoda said, "Woof, woof."

Old Freeda, with a perfect spiral, chucked old Daddy, urn and all, thirty feet into the raging river. Daddy spilled into the water and cat-a-pulted over the falls in ten thousand charred pieces. Soon Daddy was dead and buried and on his way to Nova Scotia.

Freeda's mourning ritual was interrupted by a big man wearing a red coat with shiny buttons and blue britches with a yellow stripe down the legs sitting on a great big black mother-fucking horse. He was wearin cowboy boots and a boy scout hat. He was packing heat... and the horse (my first) was twelve feet tall with a fancy leather saddle.

'HEY ma'am, Ya know you just broke the law, aye! You cannot chuck dead relatives into the river. Aye?"

Hank said, "Aye?"

The Mountie pointed to the sign, "Do not chuck dead relatives into the River. The Dead Relative Chucking Fine is $250. Aye." Freeda blushed, "Whoops."

Yoda escaped behind some shrubs to pee on a water hydrant.

While Freeda paid her fine, (Mounties take Visa and Mastercard) Slick and me and Hank wandered down the sidewalk, up the river. There was a big crowd of Asians listening to a guy who called himself "Charlie the Conjurer."

He was a fast talker, "Folks, these are illusions, not tricks! I need a volunteer to ride inside this waterproofed and shockproofed padded, metal barrel over the Falls. Aye." He pointed at a three-foot diameter, five-foot high metal barrel painted like a Canadian flag. The Asians all took two steps back. A guy, who looked like he had heard the pitch before, dressed in Canadian Flag top and the Stars and Stripes bottom stepped forward eagerly.

"Pick me Charlie the Conjurer. Aye.' He yelled. He elbowed through the crowd toward the barrel, with the open top.

Before the colorful volunteer got near the barrel, some Psycho tourorist grabbed me and Slick and tossed us inside the barrel,

"Gotcha, suckers." OMG, it was Ho, that insane Butcher from Pittsburg. (Karma bites)

Old Charlie, talkin a mile a minute, slammed the lid shut on our barrel which was loaded on a cat-a-pult to be shot into the river to go over the Falls. Slick, trapped inside the barrel with his BFF (me), looked pale and was

161

shivering in fright. Ever the observant one, I said, "Don't worry, Slick. I got this."

I had spotted the 'trapped-door' sign on the inside of the underside of the barrel... obviously an escape hatch for the 'volunteer' to use before the barrel got launched into the torrentified current of the river. I said, "We are out of here, pardner." I pulled the 'escape hatch lever'. Nothing happened. Nada! WTF!

We heard a loud 'Thwack!" and we were airborn. We landed with a jarring thud and splashing sound and felt the barrel juking down the raging river toward the falls. Then, suddenly, apart from an ear-shattering roar, everything was peaceful, like we were sailing thru the air. We were sailing thru the air!

"I don't mind flying but landing scares the crap outa me." (Slick the Tomcat) We braced for impact in the boiling cauldrum of water at the base of the falls. Death seemed certain. We were domified. Slick was saying 'Hail Marys' as fast as he could." I was saying my Buddist mantra, "Svim, Svim!" as we waited for God to intervene. Suddenly our earth-shattering fall was gradually interrupted by a series of sharp, jolting, de-accellerations. We came to a stop, jarrified, but alive, with me sitting in Slick's lap, like in 'the Madonna and Child' painting.

We had landed on "The Made of the Mist", a mafia boat that took visiting 'gangstas' for an exciting ride around the base of the Canadian Falls. Our barrel had crashed through the canvas sunroof over the back part of the boat, then crashed through a flimsy deck hatcherooni thingy and landed (thank all the gods out there) in a huge coil of rope. The 'trapped door' finally sprung open on impact.

Slick said, "Shit, kid, there goes another half-life. Running Score... Slick 6 ½ and Felix 6. It was a long walk back to Freeda and Yoda's place, and we were hurting plenty. We felt like we had been through the spin cycle of a Maytag Clothes Washer.

We slept soundly and Freeda made us a great Canadian breakfast of back bacon, Prairie-wheat pancakes, poutine and maple syrup. We all ate like lumberjacks, including Mike, who was Freeda's long-suffering husband (out of Fursona for the JW-yah sabbath). JW-yahs won't allow pets into worship... except for support parrots who can sing hymns in harmony and talking snakes.

The trip home was pretty quiet. Slick and I were pooped and slept all the way home to Pittsburg. It was great to return to the good life at the Manshun.

Chapter 20

Le Soiree de Chapelle du Renard (The Fancy Party at Fox Chapel Hill) Karma Bites Sven

"I have been thinking a lot about it and I don't think being an adult is going to work for me."

I loved my new 'Speechify Artificial Intelligence App'. I could set the output to moderately loud, sexy-woman, Americanized English voice and type in "Hey, Rosa, would ya give the cat a big bowl of cream and some salami."

Afrodite's voice boomed out from my iPad, "Hey, Rosa, would ya give the cat a big bowl of cream and some salami." Rosa obeyed like a slave, bringing me my snack.

Next I tried the Gwyneth voice... super loud. Soon Gwyneth was announcing to the entire house, "So, ladies, let's all try to put fifteen Groop Rocks in our vaginas today."

Rosa looked confused and said, "Santa madre, gracias. Pero? que son esta roca pegajajosas? Mariscos?" ("Holy Mother,Thankyou. But, what are these Groop rocks...? Seafood? (Rosettas Stones)).

A minute later Afrodite yelled downstairs, "Sorry, Gwyneth, It will only hold ten rocks. Can I put five in my mouth." Gwyneth yelled back, "Make sure you wash 'em first, sister." No wonder Gwynneth kept her lawyer on speed dial.

The festive soiree was to start at 7:00 PM. The caterers delivered all kinds of heavy Hor'durvs and foxy-moron zero-cal desserts (calorie-free whipped cream on a saltine and Splenda Frappe.)

Fifteen of V-Domes most sexy and beautiful managers showed up to be the wait-staff (for $300 cash each!). They were wearing tiny, tight black cocktail dresses with blue 'Starstuds and More' ball caps. They busily put the delishush-lookin food onto rented silver trays. The managers quickly sorted the food onto 10 different types of trays:

1. Canapes (mini sandwiches)... some smoked salmon!
2. Crudities (Raw veggies with dip with little bits of bacon in it).
3. More Yummy lookin dips with crackers and dry little toastie thingys.
4. Caviar (black fish eggs) with more little toastie thingys.
5. Sushi (Japanese treats rolled in rice or seaweed).
6. Sashimi (raw Japanese fish).
7. Little skewers (bits of meat, fish or chicken plus veggies and olives that got stabbed by a long tooth-picker).
8. Little Svedish Meatballs (Sven was coming to the soiree).
9. Little scallops (from sea shells) wrapped in cooked bacon.
10. Mini pastries... like little pies full of cheese, spinach and bacon.

The servers also set up a huge bar with every variety of booze ... everything from 16 types of crafty beer (including Bud... my favorite),vodka (4 types), Rye Whisky (Crown Royal), Bourbon (Maker's Mark, Jack Daniels and even old Pappy Van Winkle... Rips brother), Gin (Old Tom Glenever and London Dry and Slow Gin... for beginners) and yada, yada, yada... you get the drift.

Several Starstuds managers were filling tall skinny glasses (flutes) with ice cold sparkling Champlain (at $100 per bottle).

While V-Dome was upstairs changing, all the Hispanic managers and Rosa drained a coupla flutes each... and Rosa proposed a toast,

"Chicas! Este tipo es un gilipollas total con un pequeno muelle y Castor muerto en la cabeza. Pero compra buenas bebidas alcohlicas y propinas en efectivo."

(Girls! This guy is a total asshole with a little dick and a dead beaver on his head. But he buys good booze and tips in cash." Rosetta's Stones.)

Gloomer had snuck into the crowd of Latino servers and was rolling on the floor, laughing. All the Hispanic girls plus Gloomer and Rosa belted back a few more flutes to prepare for the guests.

The guests began to roll in at 7:30 pm... Goldenboy and me had hired a coupla Hell's Angels (with AK-47s) for security at the front door. We wanted the soiree to be memorable.

Soon the driveway and nearby maple-lined road was packed with big Silver SUBs (mostly Mercedees). The Sven Seven arrived fashionably late at 7:50 PM... they were excited about the fashion show. I had invited Slick and Hank to keep me company in the sunroom. Hank and Slick and me shared a half-dozen brewskis. (Bud). Goldenboy, who loved Speechify, and

Gloomer had joined us. Gloomer was wasted on champlain. Golden Boy was still sober.

The Sven Sexy Seven had all brought along
their partners or lovers (other than Sven). Most of their
partners, who were all wearing tuxedoos, were muscular
and tall and had big, white, gleaming teeth. Most of them
had really good hair, like Simon Cowell. Everyone was
drinkin champlain and air kissing and man-huggin like
crazy when the Starbuds girls started passing out the
hor'durvs. Soon, everyone was feedin their faces with as
much food as they could fit on their weenie plates. Half
the treats ended up on the floor. Slick and me did a good
job on cleanup. A whole buncha rich neighboors also
showed up. (crashers?) The sound track from the house
speakers (15 of them) played DeBussy (Arabesk), Mozart,
Choppin and orchestra string quartetified pop tunes. Mellow, dignified tunes like the Beatles.

The loud murmur of chatting Yuppies was interrupted by a tinkling dinner bell. V-Dome and Afrodite
were descending the stairs into the crowded living room
area. Everyone bust out clapping.

Afrodite was dressed in a long deep purple
Vera Wong evening dress with about three yards of extra
material trailin behind her. Most of her boobs were hanging out (cleavified). Her hair... gleaming white-blonde
and her perfect make-up made her look like she just
stepped out of a trailer (on a Hollywood Movie set). She
was clutching V-Dome's hand (never saw them touch be-

fore) and she had a huge, shiny, white smile on her gorgeous face.

V-Dome was wearing a powder blue Tux with a 'Starstuds and More' logo on both sides with "Stud" across his back. His gut was wrapped with a purple piece of Afrodite's dress called a 'Cumberbun'. He was wearing a brand-new Nordick blond wig with both a mullet and a man bun. He also had died his eyebrows and goatee white- blonde. He looked like the love child of Denarys Targarian and the Tiger King! The guests, who were getting wasted on V-Dome's free booze, clapped and hooted. The Starstuds girls, led by Rosa and Gloomer (in sweats) started chanting, "Gilipolas, Gilipolas. Darnos un aumento!" ("Asshole. Asshole. Give us a raise!" Rosetta's Stones.) V-Dome bowified and Afrodite curtsified toward the guests. The Crowd went back to guzzing champlain and scarfifying hor'durvs. All the guys had gathered in one room talkin about their cars, their yawts and their stocks.

The women had collected in the massive kitchen chatting about nannies, domestics, Butt lifts, boob jobs and Sven's carrot. The stupefying odor of pricy cologne and perfume overwhelmed a cat's olfartry system. Slick and me, after eating all the dropped smoked salmon and tasty treats off the floor, retreated to the Sunroom. Goldenboy had masterfyed Speechify... and had hooked up my iPad to the Manshun's Bluetooth speaker system. I was like Donald Rump... everyone that I associated with became an anarchist!

Sven finally arrived, unfashionably late, and jock-walked around the room, wearing a flures-cent lime green stretchy body suit featuring his muscles and, of course, his huge carrot pointing due north. His sweat socks, tidily adjusted in his crotch, faced east and west. I was a tomcat with a literal, if not a moral, compass.

Golden boy, chuckling to himself, announced Sven's arrival over the loudest setting of the manshun's speaker system. He chose the Darth Vader voice with a Svedish accent.

"Attention guests, Sven the Svede has arrived. He vill be your Commentater for ze fashion show tonite. The models vill be 'The Sven Sexy Seven' from Sven's Spa and More. The show vill start on time, or you vill be punished. Luke, you are my son."

Soon the Sven Sexy Seven began the fashion show… Afrodite was first. She swish-walked around the massive living room wiggling as much as possible without falling off her 12-inch heels. The background music was old Joe Cocker singing "I am so Beautiful!"

Sven was happy to provide the color commentary, "This Vonderful Voman is your hostess for this Vonderful soiree. She is wearing a Wera Vong original. Sorry, I got zee Wong Vang. (Humor?) Her boobs are also ze originals. She is verring Coco Mademoizel By Chanel. Give her ze applause or you vill be punished." Everyone clapped and hooted nervously.

Goldenboy added, in Sven's voice, "Lookin chubby tonite, Darlink." Goldenboy was becoming an anarchist... fast.

Afrodite gave Sven a filthy look and chucked her Cartier purple clutch at him... hitting him squarely between the eyes.

The crowd jeered and cheered and slugged back some more alcohol. Afrodite retreated to the kitchen and began to inhale a pint of Ben and Jerry's 'Moophoria Chocolate Cherry Garcia Ice Cream'. Gloomer joined her and scarfified a pint of 'Chunky Monkey'.

The fashion show continued with the Sven Seven wearing everything from Tom Ford to Ralph Lauren to Versass to Michael Coors. They all did their best to swosh around the room, but kept bumping into the guests, who were all drunk. Two of the gorgeous models got knocked off their heels onto their fannies.

Sven did his best... but kept finishing with,

"Dis member of ze Sven Seven is also looking wery chunky tonight." (a la Goldenboy and Speechify).

The seventh Sven Seven model, Tootsie Trammel, who had worked in the adult film industry, strutted her stuff last. When Sven's voice said,

"Zis beautifu voman needs to meet Chenny Craig, "(Goldenboy on Speechify)

Le Soiree de Chapelle du Renard (The Fancy Party at Fox Chapel Hill) Karma Bites Sven

Tootsie flew across the room in a rage, shrieking like a banshee, and planted a size 10 $1200 Jimmy Choo Shoe (8-inch heel) squarely into Sven's go-nads. It was a perfectly placed Carrotee kick.

By the end of the show Sven had seven large bruises on his bean (from heaved designer clutches) and the Sven Seven were all in the kitchen, seriously pissed. The 7 beauties plus Gloomer were gobblin down pints of Ben and Jerry's 2022 new flavors: Tirimasue, Salted Caramel Brownie and Strawberry Topped Tart. I ordered the treats on Amazon... delivered frozen! (No shit!) The husbands and lovers were playing beer pong in the living room, like at a frat party.

Sven limped outa the house, hanging on to his carrot, which looked broken. The Svede was fingering his giant, swollen left testacle, which had migratified north, to just below his belly button. Sven stammered, "Got to go to zee house to valk my pet Schnake, Zee Schnake Jake."

Suddenly, there was a throaty, roaring rumble of loud machinery which shook the whole manshun. The entire Chapter of the Pittsburg 'Hell's Angels' had arrived on their Harley choppers for the party. Gerry and Phil, the security bikers at the front door, had texted them about all free booze and hot chicks. Phil and Gerry emptied their AK-47s into the night air to celebrate the arrival of their 50 soul-mates.

The bearded, tattooed, middle-aged bikers with Hell's Angels cuts and grubby ponytails invaded the house. They rushed to the bar and started chugging the hard alcohol right outa the bottles.

Hank took over as DJ and started playing some line-dancing toons really loud over the manshun sound system. Golden boy as Svedish Darth Vader said, "Now you vill line-dance or you vill be punished."

Pretty soon the Hell's Angels and the Sven Seven were line- dancing to: 'Achy Breaky Heart', 'Bootin' Scootin' Boogie, Country Girl... Shake it for Me', 'Water-melon Crawl', 'Cotton Eye Joe' and 'Down in Missisippi'. The Hell's angels were pretty light on their feet and were real good at stompin'.

Hank sang a duet with Willie Nelson, 'On the Road Again'. Within a few minutes all the Guppies (rook-ie line-dancers) were stumbling around to 'the Wobble' and the 'Cha Cha Slide.' V-Dome and all the Starstuds girls were in the mix.

The party went on till six AM, when the booze ran out and some fussy neighboor called the cops. V-Dome had lost his new wig and everyone was calling him V- Dome. Afrodite and Gloomer cleaned up the last few pints of Ben and Jerry's 'Chocolate Therapy' and 'S'more Please!' ice cream. It was great to see them bondifying.

A good time was had by all. The party was a memorable success. The cleaning crew that I hired on Amazon showed up at 7 AM and took four hours to clean up the mess. Even Rosa was happy.

Le Soiree de Chapelle du Renard (The Fancy Party at Fox Chapel Hill) Karma Bites Sven

Chapter 21

The Local Sinus Fair

"Think like a proton and stay positive."—Anon

The Sunday after the party, Goldenboy showed me all the cool new developments with the Sinus Fair project.

"So, Felix, (we were texting- he knew my true Christian name, although I was sort of a Buddist.) I have mastered the mathematics and physics equations for cat flight... the path of a projectile." He rattled on about the equations for calculating flight path. Since I was the projectified tomcat, I was very interested in Time of Flight ($t = V_y/G$) and maximum height ($H = V_y^2 / 2{\times}G$). G was Gravity. In terms of maximum speed, I already knew that I could not fall at over 60 mph, because of my high surface area to weight ratio.

He added, "Do not worry, Felix, I can land you on a dime... as long as all my calculations are correct."

Goldenboy bust into song with a little regae ditty...

"In every life we have some trouble,

but when you worry you make it double.

Don't worry. Be happy" (Bobby McFerrin)

We lugged the volcano outside, with Rosa grumbling, "Ahora estos jadidos Guppies me tienen moviendo un maldito volcan. Deberia haberse quedado en Guacamole." ("Now these fucking Guppies have me moving a goddam volcano. I should have stayed in Guacamole." Rosetta's Stones).

Gloomer, who also helped with the move was sweating and cussing, "Mieda, si!" ("Shit, yeah." Rosettas Stones).

Goldenboy did five test cat-a-pult shots with a furry fake cat from Amazon that weighed the same as me (12 pounds). He hammered the tail flat to match mine and chopped off pieces from both ears to precisely match my flight profile.

He shot my 'Fursona' (I am also a Furry) outa the volcano cat-a-pult device five times and landed my 'Fursona' (Goldenboy called him 'Lucky') right on the X on the landing mat four outa 5 times. There was one dunk in the winterified swimming pool. Goldenboy was smart and I trustified him (sort of).

Slick, who had wandered over to watch the trial flights just shook his head. He was worried about me, his best friend.

The local Sinus Fair was in the high ceilinged gym (40 foot tall) of the local high school (Richfolk Regional High School) on Tuesday, so we left the volcano outside under a tarp. Rosa had started a hunger strike.

Golden boy had also perfected the chemical mix ratio of sodium bicarbonate, aqueous acetic acid and red Food Dye to create a robust salava flow from the mouth of the volcano. By pushing buttons labelled 1, 2 and 3 Goldenboy could release up to three cannisters of each the potent chemicals to create the red Salava explosion. He explained that one cannister was good, two cannisters were 'bit bold', and three cannisters were 'Right Outa Sight'.

Slick was still shaking his head and murmured, "Why can't we just chase dogs for fun?" Slick was not into the sinuses like I was.

On Tuesday, Hank very kindly agreed to transport Goldenboy, me, Slick, the Volcano, the cameras, the poles and all the computer stuff to the high school. I had augmentified my flight suit with a silver cervical spine protector collar (Amazon) and four mini silver boots to protect my four paws. They looked excellent, matching my silver helmut with a pull-down face shield (like the race car drivers), my silver cape and my reflective silver sunglasses (to be cool). Silver brought out the best in my sleek coat and made me look edgy. The judges soon arrived at our exhibit.

My work on the reflex light machine was stellar... reaction time down to .04 seconds (normal cats are .10 seconds). Slick refused to be the 'Control untrained cat'. Who could blame him.

Next came the volcano with my cat-a-pulted space flight. Goldenboy was operating both the cat-a-pult crank, the cat ejectiflying button, and the buttons (1,2 and 3) for lava flow. The judges were Biology teachers from the Community College. Goldenboy gave them a detailed speech about cat-flight and righting reflexes, including the equations and calculations.

Goldenboy helped me don my flying gear... sun glasses, silver helmut, neck brace, cape and silver boots. The judges applauded loudly and put their hands over their hearts. Slick waved goodbye and Hank crossed himself. Goldenboy cranked the cat-a-pult rubber bands to 'medium', and activated the twelve cameras (Motion detected). Goldenboy hit button 1 to start the salava flow. I braced myself in the cockpit. I heard the chemicals reacting and bubbling in the salava chamber in base of the volcano. Salava poured outa the volcano and down the mountainside toward me.

Goldenboy hit the 'Launch Button' and I was ejectified into the air headfirst, waving at the judges as I flew by toward the gym ceiling. In about three seconds I hit the apogee (top point) of my flight (32 feet) and headed back down toward the gym floor where Goldenboy had placed a padded mat with a big X in the middle. I nailed the landing on four silver-booted paws. I grinned at the judges. Goldenboy decided to skip the Flight with Catnip phase since the judges were already pushing the huge Sinus Fair Regional Grand Champion Trophy in our direction.

Our advancement to the East Coast Invitational Sinus Fair at Harvard University, in Boston, in two weeks was guaranteeified! We all celebrated at McDonald's on the way home. I liked the quarter pounder... no bun, no cheese, no gas. Slick had a McFish Fillet... no cheese, no bun, still gas. Slick and I drank a Vanilla milk shake outa the trophy. Goldenboy and Hank hammered down Big Macs with glee. Hank volunteered to take us to Harvard if we need a ride.

Chapter 22

Harvard at Last

The trip down to Boston with Slick, Goldenboy, Hank and me in the Ford 150 shitbox was really fun. Hank was singing Wilie Nelson with Goldenboy, who had a decent voice. Slick and me purred along, backing up the choruses. Our best tunes were 'Always on My Mind,' and, of course, 'On the Road Again.'

We also did some Roy Orbison. Slick and me were amazing in the wailing part of 'Crying Over You.' Hank had tears in his eyes and Goldenboy was yelling, "Bravo, Bravo!" by the time we wound it up.

We had all our scientific gear in the back of the shitbox truck covered with tarps. We would be in Boston over the weekend, staying in a Harvard dorm. Pittsburg to Boston was a long way... 572 mile (9-10 hours).

We stopped a few times for snacks and pee breaks. I discovered Subway Tuna Salad which was decent.

Hank and Goldenboy were having the same old Hank and Hank discussion, except they took turns asking and answering.

Hank, "Why is Donald Rump such an asshole?"

Goldenboy, "Duh! He was born that way. Besides, his name is Rump!"

Goldenboy, "Who is the most honest politician in America?"

Hank, "Duh! There aren't any."

This biting satire and banter went on for two hours while Slick and I napped. The winner of the Eastern regional Sinus Fair would be awarded the East Coast Cup and, also, a free scholarship to Harvard. Goldenboy was now twelve. I had no intentions of wasting my mind at college. But, we agreed that it would be great to win. We had wangled a credit card outa V-Dome, who had found his new blond wig in the punch bowl. (Whoops!). It was now a striking strawberry-blondified hairpiece. He had died his goatee and eyebrows to match. Rosa quit her hunger strike after she missed a meal.

We rolled into Harvard about midnight and we all crashed in the small dorm room which smelled of weed. I was pumped about being at the famous place... following in the boots of John F. Kennedy, John Adams,

Franklin and Teddy Roosevelt (Brothers), Barrack Obama, and of course a few dummies like George F. Bush (who studied Phys-ed). We went to the cafeteria in the morning for bacon and cream. (Yummy)

We headed over to the Faculty of Veterinary Science, where we would exhibit Part One of the Sinus Project on Friday. Goldenboy now called Part One, 'Cat reflexes and Intelligence. Do Cats have a Sense of Humor?"

Part Deux was now (ominously) called, "Cat Righting Reflexes and Spacial Sense while Flying," and would be presented at the Hockey Arena on Saturday. Goldenboy had scrapped the catnip.

I had researched the judges online, a coupla Harvard Faculty PhD Veterinary Doctors who were married to each other. The guy was Simon Llewellen Underhill-Trent, PhD, MSc, BVSc. He was Perfesser Emeritus of the Department of Sub-Humanoid Vertebrate Mammals. His student on 'Yelp' all described him as 'an arrogant asshole' and the students all called him Dr. SLUT (his initials).

The woman, also a Harvard perfesser, was Nanook Underwood-Trent-Sloan, PhD, MSc, BVSc who was a Cat Psychiatrist in The Department of Sub-Humanoid Vertebrate Psychiatric Wellness (or not). Her Yelp student reviews described her as 'a Caring, arrogant asshole who was good listener.' The students all called her 'Dr. Nuts." (her initials).

We spent all morning setting up Part One, "Cat Reflexes and Intelligence. Do cats have a Sense of Humor?" The Reflex part involved the coloured panel thingy and the Velcroed drumstick tappers. The second part involved me telling and hearing jokes (via Speechify... which I knew would knock the judges socks off).

For Part One, both Goldenboy and me wore classy Crimsom and Black Harvard academic gowns... those black sacky things that made you look like you joined a choir, with Motorboat hats on our heads (like half a pizza box with a little tassal hanging off).

We practiced a bit, then had some lunch, ready for the show to start. At about 2 PM the judges, Dr. SLUT and DR. Nuts approached our exhibit.

Dr. Nuts was a 60ish matronly-looking woman, wearing a crimson and black academic gown (minus the headgear), looking pretty friendly and interesting. She had one asthma inhaler thingy in each hand. The air quality in Boston sucked.

Dr. SLUT, with a huge white, unkemptified beard (like Santa Claws but much chubbier) had a huge gut. He waddled up to the exhibit... ten feet behind his wife. He was wheezing but she wouldn't lend him her inhaler...

"Hygiene, hygiene, Dear. Have you forgotten about Covid, you twat," she explained, with a scowl.

185

Goldenboy introduced me as "Felix the Tomcat" from the mean streets of Pittsburg who was a self-taught cat progidy who had wandered into his life to find culture and education and had mastered the internet and had his own iPad. Talk about a run-on sentences.

Editors Note: I am the editor, asshole.

Felix's Note: No, you are the asshole, editor. You're fired!

Dr. Nuts said, "Very interesting." And Dr. Slut coughed, "Bullshit!"

I performed on the round coloured-panel thingy showing my lightening cat-like reflexes (down to .035 seconds). A crowd of students had gathered to watch my prowess. (Looked like Niagara Falls, Canada... all Asians except for three geeky-lookin white guys and two black women). They were all makin movies of me on their iPhones.

Arthurs Note: If I have not insulted your race, religion, sex, group or club please email me at felixthetomcat2022@outlook.com (I am an equal opportunity offender).

The crowd went wild clapping and hooting after seeing my lightening reflexes.

Goldenboy set up the 'Speechify App hooked up to speakers and my iPad. My typing entries were shown on a 54" flat screen TV. He helped me put iPad Velcroed Stylish Pens on both my paws. I practiced on

'Speechify' in the deepest, booming Morgan Freedom voice,

"Hello, Harvard. This is God... testing, testing, testing." The voice boomed outa the speakers. The crowd had grown to at least two hundred souls. They loved Morgan.

I continued after doing a little happy dance on stage. I stuck to the old Morgan Freedom voice. My paws were flying on the iPad.

"A cat, a Doberman and a Labrador Retriever die and go to Heaven. Saint Peter meets them at the Pearly Gates and takes them in to meet God, who is sitting in a golden throne between two smaller silver thrones.

God looked at the Golden Retriever and said, "I want to know why you believe you should be admitted to Heaven."

The Golden Retriever says, "I always wagged my tail and was loyal to my Master."

God pointed to the the silver throne on His right side and said,

"Good doggie. Sit!"

Then God looked at the Doberman and said. "And why should you be admitted to Heaven?"

The Doberman scratched a few fleas and responded, "I have been a dependable guard dog and a loyal companion for my masters, the Hell's Angels, all my life.

God pointed to the throne on his left and said,

"Good doggie, Sit!"

Finally, God looked at the cat, who was grooming himself, ready for Heaven. God said, in his booming, bass voice,

"And you, pussy, what makes you think you belong in Heaven?

The cat rolled his eyes, looking pissed,

"First of all, don't ever call me 'Pussy' and secondly,

Get outa my chair!"

The crowd was in Hysterics. Dr. Nuts was slapping her knee and howling with laughter. Dr. SLUT was in afroplexy… wheezing and laughing like he was about to expire on the spot. Hank was killing himself guffawing in his deep husky voice. Slick was rolling around the ground with his high-pitched giggle. I giggled nervously and slapped my knee a few times.

Golden boy, in his most formal voice announced, over the speaker system,

"And that, Harvard, is why I believe that cats have a sense of humor."

A few of the Asians, chuckling politely, were explaining the joke to their friends. We hit the 'Lucky Fortune Buffet' for supper and had a stroll down the Charles River beside Harvard. Slick and I ate some field mice, a wimpified squirrel (grey) and a coupla emaciafied rats. We all had an early night to prepare for the flight/volcano portion of our presentation.

Chapter 23

Felix Flies and Stromboli Expodes

"One small step for a Tomcat, One giant leap for the Universe." (Felix)

I was sleeping when Goldenboy nudged me awake,

"Hey Felix… '#FelixtheTomcatStandup' is trending on Instagram with 250,000 hits since 3 PM. You have gone viral."

OMG, I hoped I wasn't infectified with the Hankivirus or Chlamydia or PTSFD. I frowned. Goldenboy pulled the viral recording of my Standup performance on Instagram. I loved it… it was funny. Ya gotta love a cat with the Morgan Freedom voice.

Goldenboy said, "Relax Felix. It's all good PR for the Sinus Fair tomorrow. Could you get together 15 minutes of standup comedy to open for me before the Volcano/ Cat-Takes-Flight show?" I nodded. For a Tomcat with a hyperthymesified memory, 15 minutes of jokes was like singing 'Twinkle, Twinkle'. My problem was to forget all the bad jokes I heard, especially on late night TV.

We all had a great sleep and went off for a hearty bacon and cream breakfast. At about 11 AM we went to the Harvard Hockey Arena to set up all our scientific gear. Hank was able to drive the F150 shitbox up close to the arena to unload the volcano and poles (not the central Europeeans). Goldenboy had trained Hank to control the volcano eruptify buttons, to ease performance stress on himself.

Soon the whole setup was ready, including my iPad hooked up to the speakers, Speechify and the giant TV screen... in case Goldenboy needed an opening act. We wandered off to Subway for lunch and me and Slick shared a virgin footlong Tuna salad sub (no cheese, no bun) and a quart of Homo Milk.

When we returned to the arena at 1:40 PM, every damn seat in the place was full: Harvard students in Crimson sweatshirts, faculty, and a ton of teenagers all chantifying in unisom, "Felx! Felix! Felix! Jokes! Jokes! Jokes!"

OMG! I was stupefied! I quickly put on my silver cape and silver boots. Goldenboy strapped my iPad stylishes to my front Paws. I wore a tiny Harvard ball cap (backwards), and moon-walked up to the mike on stage,

"Hey, Harvard! Whassup? Whassap?"

The crowd went nuts, whistling and cheering… chanting, "Jokes, Jokes, Jokes! Fe-LiX, Fe-LiX, Fe-LiX!"

I switched the Speechify App to Morgan Freedom with a max bass voice and typed like crazy… 300 words a minute. (normal speech is 140-170 words per minute.)

Morgan's modulated bass voice boomed through the speakers, "A tough, three-legged, Texas Tomcats walked into a bar wearing six-shooters , cowboy boots and a Stetsome hat. The bartender looked up and said, "How can I help you, pardner?" The big cat spoke in a deep Texas drawl, "I'm lookin for the guy who shot my paw."

The crowd howled and Hank and Slick gave me encouraging waves. I kept typing like crazy and left the voice on Morgan Freedom …

"So, a mother took her teenage girl to a psychiatrist." The psychiatrist said.

"What is the problem with your daughter?

The mom replied, "She is a Furry… she thinks she is a cat!."

The psychiatrist said, "Hmm. Interesting. When did she start thinking she was a cat."

Mom replied, "Ever since she was a kitten!"

Every seat in the hockey arena was full and the crowd was goin nuts. I could see Dr. Nuts and Dr.SLUT elbowing their way through the frantic crowd toward our exhibit. All the other exhibitors had given up and had gathered to watch the show!

Goldenboy held up a finger and mouthed, "One More!" Morgan gave them a Harvard -style one-liner,

"Did you hear that Schroedinger's cat is wanted… Dead or Alive." (for intellectuals only)

Only the physics and philosophy students laughed hard and everyone else laughed, because every-one else was laughing.

Dr. SLUT was laughing, "Ho-ho-Ho!" I chuck-led. I gave them an old chestnut to wrap up my gig. Mor-gan said,

"A rabbi, a Hindu, and a lawyer are in a car that breaks down in the countryside one evening. They walk to a nearby farm and the farmer tells them that he has only two beds and one of them will have to sleep in the barn.

The Hindu volunteers because he has humility. A few minutes later and says, "Sorry, I cannot sleep in a building with a cow."

So, the rabbi volunteers, trying to be helpful. He soon returns saying," Sorry, I cannot sleep in a building with a pig."

So, the lawyer, grumbling, has to sleep in the barn. Ten minutes later, the pig and the cow come to the door."

I bowified toward deafening whoops and cheers. My first stand-up. I moon-walked over to Goldenboy to don the rest of my flying gear.

Dr. SLUT, still laughing, gave us a thumbs up, "You may commence the experiment." He was not wheezing today. Dr. Nuts looked relaxed and pleasant, again wearing her academic gown.

I was fully prepared for flight in my: silver helmut with face shield, reflective sunglasses, silver neck brace, silver cape and silver boots. The crowd applauded feverishly as I moon-walked back to the Volcano. Goldenboy gently lifted me into the 10-inch diameter cat-a-pult hatch on the side of the volcano hidden from the crowd. It was padded, clean and cozy.

While I braced myself, I heard Goldenboy say, "Ok, Hank, push button number One to erupt the volcano." I heard chemicals splashing and rumbling deep inside the volcano base.

The reaction seemed quite robust today... red, bubbling salava was shooting fifty feet into the air and falling down into my hatch.

Goldenboy was yelling, "Hank! I said button number one!"

Hank, who was pretty deaf, said,

"I thought you said, Push one button. Hey, I like three."

The volcano was shakin and heavin exactly like Mount Stromboli, Goldenboy poked the 'Ejectify button'- to get me out of danger. Now, that is irony!

The orientation of the Volcano had shifted with the massive eruption, and I was shot 65 feet in the air at the apogee. Meanwhile, red saliva had invaded the judges table, knocking Dr. Nuts and Dr. SLUT off their chairs onto their backs on the floor. The bubbly red salava had also flowed to completely engulfify the first ten rows of folding chairs set up for visiting VIPs like parents, scientists and Harvard Alumni.

After my parabolified path peaked, I started to descend at sixty miles an hour. I realized that I was going to overshoot the landing mat with the X in the center.

Nauseated with fear, I began to puke and may have soiled myself. Directly below me was the supine form of Dr. SLUT, on his back, partially buried in seething red bubbly salava. His gut stretched beneath me like the flight deck of the USS Gerald R. Ford (Americas biggest aircraft carrier… Google).

I crashed, on my paws mind you, moving at maximum velocity, into Dr. SLUT's huge rotundified bread-basket. He puked and then I puked (again and again). Then Dr Nuts, who was also on her back immersed in red Salava, also puked. Even some of the VIP's puked. It was not pretty. Hank had disappeared. The crowd in the Hockey Arena loved the show.

The janitorial crew cleaned up the huge mess after the judges left the building; Doctor SLUT (by ambulance) and Doctor Nuts slip-sliding through the slick salava. There were still a few fans chanting, "Fe-Lix. Joke! Fe-Lix. Joke! Fe-Lix, Joke!" but the mood in the place had changed.

The judges results would be presented Sunday morning at 11 AM. We all went back to the dorm for a shower (A good lick for me and Slick… we licked out each other's ears) and then we hit the Chinese Buffet again for supper. The shrimp egg rolls were tasty and I loved the eel. We all agreed that we had given it our best shot.

By bedtime, '#FelixtheTomcatStandup' was trending #1 on Instagram, Reddit and TicToc with

100,000,000 hits and '#HarvardBlowedUPbyCatandKid' was trending #2 with 67,000,000 hits. We were famous.

Chapter 24

The Awards Ceremony (Dr. SLUT gets PTSFD)

"I took the speed reading course and read 'War and Peace' in twenty minutes. It's about Russia." — Woody Allen

Dr. Nuts appeared on the main lecture hall stage at the Faculty of Veterinary Medicine at 11 AM sharp. Her skin had a healthy pink glow (red food dye) and she was wearing a clean Crimson academic gown. She stepped up to the mike.

"Good morning competitors and parents, Honorable Faculty and Harvard students. Yesterday was a blast!" Everyone laughed.

"Sorry, our beloved Dr. SLUT has been admitted to the psychiatry ward of Massachessetts General Hospital with advanced cata-tonia. (another laugh). It is unclear if the ultimate diagnosis will be PTSFD (Post-Traumatic Fucking Stress Disorder) or Hysteria." She winked...

'The boy can be a Wuss!" She was a good standup, too.

She continued in a more serious vein, "It is so difficult to decide who made the best impression on us as judges this year. But after careful thought and a couple hours of Cognitive Therapy (she winked again),"... another laugh...

"Here are the winners!" She held up a piece of pink paper (Salava damaged I guessed).

For first prize in the Eastern US Regional Middle School Sinus Fair... (there was a drum roll... No Shit!)

"Felix the Tomcat... for Best Standup Comedy and Smartest Cat in the World." She shoved the huge golden metal 'East Coast Gold Cup' toward me.

It looked like Shaq's Jockstrap's cup. Fun Fact... Shaq donated it to Harvard when he was playing for Miami... he hated the Boston Celtics that much!

"Felix will be offered a Faculty position at Harvard in the brand new, innovative Faculty of Super-

Humanoid Vertebrate Mammals. I will be the new Professor Emeritas.

Felix will require a psychiatric assessment with an illustrious Cat Psychiatrist, Dr. Nanook-Underwood Trent-Sloan, PhD, MSc, BVSc. (She was her pointing index finger at her own brain, Winking and mouthing 'ME!') This psychiatric evaluation is necessary to prevent mental illness slipping through the gates of this hallowed Ivory Tower… again."

She winked again… maybe just a nervous tick or maybe the onset of Tourette's. She continued, twitching,

"And second prize and this gorgeous East Coast Silver Cup (which looked like LeBron's silver Jock strap cup… and, in fact, was Lebron's cup… he also hated the Celtics), is awarded to 'Goldenboy' Shultz a fine grade 8 student from suburban Pittsburg, Pennsylvania. His extraordinary work on cat humor, cat reflexes, cat irony, cat intelligence and cat flight will be rewarded with a four-year full-ride Harvard Scholarship, when he gets out of high school." She blinked a few more times and muttered "Son of a Bitch" to herself three times… (it was Tourette's). She continued,

"Goldenboy will also have the honour of co-writing a scientific paper with me. She was pointing at her brain and blinking again. A paper on our ground-breaking discovery of high intelligence, humor and irony in felis

felis (Tomcats)." The crowd, about 1000 of them, applauded and hooted.

Slick, Hank, Goldenboy and me, complete with the East Coast Silver and Gold Cups, headed back to the Chinese Buffet for lunch before my Cat Psychiatry evaluation at 1 PM in Dr. Nuts' private office at Harvard. I swear, those eels were addictifying for both me and Slick. Slick and I drank cream out of our victory jock strap cups trophies.

Chapter 25

My Psychiatry Evaluation (Confidential)

"The more I get to know people, the more I understand why Noah only took animals on the ark."

I wore my silver cape and Harvard ballcap (backwards) to my psychiatry evaluation with Dr. Nuts. (ironic dress code)

After lying down on the hard couch, I hooked up my iPad to Speechify and typed like crazy. I opened the session in the Darth Vader's voice,

"Did you hear the one about Darth Vader and the shrink? Darth Vader complained of having 'Daddy issues.'

The psychiatrist asked, 'Darth, you poor dear, how long have you had these problems?"

Darth said, "Ever since I got drunk at the Supreme Galactic Council Christmas party and said, "Luke, you are my son!"

Dr. Nuts chuckled, then took the lead, asking me all kinds of questions, which I answered in the 'Gwyneth Pulcritude' voice (She has a lawyer on speed-dial).

Dr. Nuts did the basic psych assessment;

Q: "Are you nuts."

A: "Sometimes."

Q: "Do you ever feel frightened?"

A: I lied, "Rarely, I am a Pittsburg   Tomcat."

Q:" Do you like me?"

A: I lied. "I love you. You have a future in standup… or science. Either one!"

Q: "Do you see things that are not there?"

A:" Like rainbows and TV? Yup."

Q: "Do you hear voices in your head?"

A: "No, through my ass. Just jokin!"

Q: "Are you erudite enough to teach University at Harvard?"

A: "I lick myself every day and my strokum twice a day. Geez, Louise!"

Q: "Do you have any bad habits?"

A: "None that I can tell you about".

Q: "What is your favorite pastime?"

A: "Coitus, followed by ratting and mousing, bird killing and terrorizing dogs".

Q: "Really, Do you like me?"

A: "I used to but the urge is passing."

Q: "If you came to work for me at Harvard, what would your salary need to be?"

A: "Hmmm. A million a year would peakify my interest."

I had read about Harvards' $50.9 BILLION endowment Fund. She beamed a smile, "Wow, Dr. Felix the Tomcat, you are hired! You will receive an Honorary Harvard Phd and can start in a week."

Gwyneth asked politely, "Now, Dr. Nuts, what would you expect of me as a faculty member?"

DR. Nuts explained, "Well, Dr. Felix, once you move to Boston to live in your free faculty housing, we would have you castrated as soon as feasible. It is an inflexible Harvard Veterinary school policy to neuter all Tomcats on Campus."

Gwyneth stammered, "I could send my lectures in by Facetime from Pittsburgh. That's home."

Dr. Nuts, who was by this time, staring at my go-nads, said, "No, sorry Felix, here at Harvard we like to be down close and intimate with both students and faculty."

Shaking my head vigorously I put on the Darth Vader voice to give her a famous quote:

"Powerful you have become, the dark side I sense in you." (Yoda) In Gwynneth's sweetest voice, I added, "Now I understand why they call you Dr. Nuts." I jumped off the shrink's couch and moon-walked out of the room, hanging on to my precious go-nads. Live free or die.

Chapter 26

On the Road again

*"Dogs come when they are called. Cats take a message
and get back to you later."*—*Mary Bly.*

*"On the road again like a band of gypsies we go down
the highway*

We're the best of friends

Insisting that the word keep turning our way

And our way

Is on the road again"—*Willie Nelson.*

Slick, me, Hank and Goldenboy headed back to Pittsburg in the F150 shitbox early Monday morning.
Slick and me agreed that the Harvard sheenanigans

had cost me another half-life. So Slick and me were both at 7 ½ lives (getting tight).

Goldenboy was thrilled that he could go to Harvard... if he felt like it. He thought Dr. Nuts was trying to steal the academic credit for all his hard work. However, Goldenboy had already been approached by famous PHds at Cal Tech, Stanford, Yale, Cornell, Rutgers, and MIT to co-study cat intelligence and humor. Opa Windfree wanted me and Goldenboy to appear on her show. Tenn and Peller wanted me to open for them in Vegas. Yada, yada, yada.

Me and Slick could not wait to get back home for some serious mousing and ratting and some serious coitus with hornifyed Queens in heat.

As evening fell there was a golden sunset in the west over the rollified blue Allegany Mountains as we rolled home to Pittsburg.

THE END

Arthur's Note: Is this really the end of Felix the Tomcat? Or… will Felix the Tomcat and his gang re-emergify to set off on new, exciting escapades in the near future. Sorry, folks if I have taken livertease with the English language… relax, I am a quick study.

Felix and M.P. Frank website is FelixtheTomcat2022.blog

Leave a book review at Amazon.com. Thanks.

The Nine Lives of Felix the Tomcat

Made in the USA
Middletown, DE
04 May 2023

29961035R00126